FLASH FICTION III

OTHER VANTAGE PRESS TITLES BY THE AUTHOR:

Flash Fiction

Flash Fiction II

FLASH FICTION III

Craige Reeves

✿ VANTAGE Press

This is a work of fiction. Any similarity between the names and characters in this book and any real persons, living or dead, is purely coincidental.

Cover design by

FIRST EDITION

All rights reserved, including the right of reproduction in whole or in part in any form.

Copyright © 2011 by Craige Reeves

Published by Vantage Press, Inc.
419 Park Ave. South, New York, NY 10016

Manufactured in the United States of America
ISBN: 978-0-533-16096-9

Library of Congress Catalog Card No: 20089906350

0 9 8 7 6 5 4 3 2 1

FLASH FICTION III

WALTER AND MOLLY

The holidays were coming. Christmas. New Year's. Chanukah. *Kwanza;* and a host of others. For Walter Chronticus; the holidays were going to be grim—grim indeed. The day he had slid Molly, his eighteen wheeler, burning rubber off the turnpike, there was no one in his truck other than Walter who was yelling about World Wide Glacier trouble; Grim holidays. But a curse will endure through good times and bad, too bad for that Self-Proclaimed ole Randy-Assed Trucker; Walter Chronticus too!

"Joy to the World" doesn't apply to the good folk lugging a curse around with them like some kind of amulet! No. No. No. As we look in on our Randy-Assed Trucker, Walter R. Chronticus, we see his feverish maneuvering of Molly. Eighteen wheels of burning rubber closing on that Humvee. We think; military. We think of the similar appearance of this low-to-road slung ten wheeler; yeah, yeah, like a 'Bradley'! Run Bradley; Run! Outdistance this hunk of road turd bearing down on you for all the world like it isn't in the least interested in maintaining a safe distance between vehicles during busy holiday traffic. Run Bradley Run! We like the contest.

It makes our hearts palpitate just ever so much more slightly; quicker. We can live with that. Our fingers begin to tap a slight tempo, on our own steering wheels as we hang back enough to be 'no nuisance' if the big guy in the semi backs off on the petrol a little. No matter what the beat goes on!!! The blatant blare of twin air horns situated on both sides of the top of the truck top makes your mid midsection grip. The fucking guy is crazy. You just know the guy in the Humvee just shit himself. Ummmh. The Randy-Assed Trucker in The Eighteen Wheeler named 'Molly'—is winning.

We really don't KNOW what the guy in the truck is doing—or why—or if he's losing control—going ape-shit but we can figure he ain't dealing from a full deck. ... Now he must have pulled the wheel down to the right while riding the brakes 'cause the body of Molly is sliding perpendicular-like down the road. We're getting a show alright and all it cost is the fare at the toll at the other end. And don't we feel a little bad about Humvee? Nah!

THE STUDENT

Archie was walking up the silent street whistling tunelessly. It was Two A.M. Arthur J. Hock had the 'Heebee-Jeebees'. It was the sound he had heard two blocks back where the old McCoy house used to be. It'd been part growl/part howl. Archie kept looking back over his shoulder.

The night was dark. There was no moon out and this far up Manor Street there weren't many streetlights. The dead lot of the old McCoy house beckoned. Go back? Go in the excavated cellar? Sure jump on in you knucklehead. You hairbrained idiot. Maybe you won't land on a board with rusty nails poking on up out of it. Maybe it won't rain while you're down there; eroding the sides of the cellar as you uselessly try to claw your way; up and out!

But what if the growl/howl was a dog some punk threw down there? Arthur J. Hock stopped in mid-step away from the empty tenements leading back to the McCoy house; turned and reluctantly re-traced his steps. The growling was louder. Do I want to do this? Creeping closer to the edge of the basement Archie peered into dark gloom. He was unable to see what was in the hole; but apparently it saw his contour against the sky. It yelped a little now that it was discovered. Arthur thought, *if I go down; and try to help it will it bite me?* He thought not. He looked around. There was a sheet of plywood lying nearby that would serve as a ramp. Carefully placing the ramp in the hole, Archie jumped in. He fell on *no* board with rusty nails poking on up out of it.

As soon as Arthur J. Hock was in the excavation, the dog jumped up and down near Arthur's leg, licking like it was a bowl of water. As Arthur was trying to persuade the dog to walk up the plywood and out of the hole, taking a step or two up it himself.

He even pushed gently on the dog's butt. The moon glowed through the clouds and the dog metamorphosed into a werewolf.

NAUGHT

Was it all for naught? Or was I losing my mind? I couldn't seem to make heads or tails out of what day it was let alone give a weather report. I mean after all yes, I was hit in the back, by that speeding car and yes, it had left tire tracks up one side of me and down the other. But c'mon.
    I was lying on Forbes Ave. When I say I was lying on Forbes Ave., brother, you better believe I was lying ON Forbes Ave. And, yeah I felt like I had been half pushed through Forbes Ave. But after all ... Anyway, I thought I should be screaming. Someone who is hit in the back by a speeding car screams. Screams their frickin' head off. Ya' know what I was doing? I was laughing. I was laughing fit to beat the band! And you say, someone who is hit in the back should be screaming 'fit to beat the band'—and here you are laughing. Laughing 'fit to beat the band'!
    I could see the car that hit me. It was askant in the street. A Luv Bug. That's what they called 'em. Luv Bugs. Well; this 'Luv Bug' wiped me out. And I couldn't get over it. A crowd had gathered and I was at an angle on Forbes Ave. LOOKING AT THE 'Bug' that did me in, laughing my damn fool head off. 'Ya see; I'd won the lottery. I'd won the lottery. And I'd registered the ticket, and I was on my way across Forbes Ave. that soon becomes Myers Boulevard. And then Highway 101; and I got creamed. I had after registering the ticket, opened a huge bank account. The reason for the haste across Forbes Ave.? To buy a car.

THE BEAT

"Pa-Dum" "Pa-Dum" "Pa-Dum." The beat goes on; Henry TONE thought Riley. "Pa-Dum." "Pa-Dum." "Pa-Dum." As well as hearing this cadence in his mind, Henry Tone counted each and every 'beat' of the words. Maybe the counting each part of this brainwork wasn't entirely accurate. To maintain the tempo of a cadence while counting ever single beat, didn't seem possible—even to Henry Tone; and he was the one trying to do it.

So let's say Henry has a load of wash in the machine; does he count revolutions of the washer? NO. maybe says; "Per"-"Dum"-"Per"-"Dum" between what our mystery man guesses is between seconds. This is not at all easy. It's kinda like makin' your heart skip a beat. Like trying to hold your breath every other one—long enough to say; "Per"-"Dum"-"Per"-"Dum"—in a synchronized way.

Do I have to tell you how long a load of laundry takes? Do I need to tell you how long it takes to do a load of dishes???

No; sometimes Henry Tone lies in the fetal position in his bed moaning; "Why?" "Why...???"

HARVEY

Harvey was shuffling his feet up the road. A dirt road. A dusty dirt road that had no shoulders. So that let's say some '44 Dodge come rumblin' by, Harvey would have to toe the mark. Leave the dirty dusty side of the road he was shufflin' on; not curse, not curse; his Pa tol' Harvey to his dyin' day, "Don't curse, Harvey; don't curse."

The sun was bright. The type of day Harvey told his three-year-old girlfriend, Shelley, "If ya' squint yer' eyes and leave 'em open a tiny bit; you can see; different colors. Or if you rub your eyes and open them suddenly; you see bright colors too." So anyway; Harvey was walking up the same dusty, dirty road he always did; only this time there was something blue glowing, maybe ten feet off to the side of the road. At first Harvey figured it was one of those Etch-A-Sketch games. Special blue model; thank you very much.

He moved closer to get a good look. It was blinking. It was the size of a shoe box and it was blue. And it was blinking. Kazamm. Tell a fool not to pick up a blinking, shoebox-sized blue box. Harvey bent and lifted his new toy. Uh Oh.

Pain; bad pain hot up Harvey's arms. They began to shrink as Harvey screamed. He was on a lonely, dusty, dirty road. No one heard him. His hands shrunk up to his sleeves and began to climb up inside them. His legs began to creep up his pants.

So Harvey began to think. Don't shuffle. No, don't shuffle your dumb feet. But Harvey was shriveling. No, Harvey wouldn't shuffle his feet anymore. There was no more Harvey after a bit.

FULL CIRCLE

October 31st. Halloween. Full Moon. Whole Moon. Witch's Moon. Light mist. Chilly. Windless. The houses are dark. Pa has to go to the plant in the morning. He's been asleep for hours. Ma tossed and turned; in troubled sleep. Iraq? Gas prices? It was alright for me.

When the house quieted, I went downstairs and put on a pot of coffee. I'd written four books. Maybe I'd write tonight.

The moon was also what I called: 'A Writer's moon.' I thought, I wrote a letter in a jungle by moonlight. Pretty fanciful.

I take medicine. Sometimes I joke around and say something like, "I take medicine to keep YOU safe." I'm close. I'm close to learning what my full potentials are. I joke about that, too. I'll invariably say something like, "A testosterone-induced coma. Pass the phenerimones." I feel so pumped sometimes; I feel like I'm going to jump right out of my skin. That I'm on a 'Nat-ural *bent* of steroids.'

I get the Hee-Bee Jee-Bees though. Quiver. Shake like I got the flu. Nerve damage. Shouldn't have mentioned Jungle. Brain Lesions? Synapses? Motor Control of Left/Right, Right/Left Hemispheres?

The fireflies were big tonight. I kept smacking them. Crushing them. Bashing them.

Oh! Those were Pumpkins with candles inside!

THE CURSE

My buddy swears. Swearing my buddy does. He can no more keep from saying, "Chuck you Farley" in so many words; as, "What the ^%^%^ is eating you?" When I look at him, I'm succinct. If brutal. "Cancer."
"Poor Jonesey. He's got the bug. Now the rest of you can drop dead; eat &$&$$#, and bark at the moon."
"No, Johnny. What I got I got. And that's my tough ^^$$*I ()_; But I think about Judgment Day. Judgment Day? Judgment Day? What the **(&^^% is 'Judgment Day'?
He hurried on, "It's a 'Friggin' Crock 'O Canary Carrion!" Wait. Wait. What is this? What did Johnny just say? That didn't register. It was way off the charts.
"Johnny, calm down, man." He was turning purple, foaming at the corners of his mouth; and he had a big green vein in his right eye. I was backing away from Johnny at this point because, he was about to collapse. I was about to go stark raving mad myself. And I could smell stuff. Used matches and rotten eggs. Farts and egg shells, Ma used to say. My eyes watered.
Johnny was backing away from me too. He knew what it was. Judgment Day. He began to twitch like he had St. Vidas Disease. He began to jerk like he was a puppet on a string. He soiled himself. He sicked up. His eyes bulged. I was trying to show a little compassion and NOT stare, but you know one of the last things Johnny ever said to me was, "DON'T EYE-BALL ME!"

BRANDED

Two down on the left past Brandon. The guy had stopped moaning and twitching like a Jack-A-Lope with its big ears grabbed up. Of course the guy two down on the left was strung up by wife. His hands were tied to the big, thick metal rings with wire. Me and Brandon were tied up with rope.

Cigars were held on us. Shoved in us. We screamed. We bucked. We burned. Yes, we burned. At least we were alive. Barely. Brandon was going insane. Asked for cigarettes. Coffee. And Brandon burned. I burned and I screamed, and I hung in their dungeon. And I pretended I was going insane. I made myself spit up on myself; like I was insane with fear.

I was scared. I was worried. But I was NOT insane with fear. I tried to get a little info out of the guy next to Brandon. Brandon was still at the moment.

"Who's that?" I was indicating the corpse being gnawed on by rats at the base of the wall. "Friend." That helped.

"Where are you from, mister?" I decided tough was better. He bristled. "Jamaica."

"Why are we here?"

"Those Towel-Heads—think they're supposed to torture us to death. Muhammad. Allah."

He answered my question before I even asked it.

"How long have you been here, buddy?"

"An hour. Ten years."

A heavy key rattled in the lock. A guard came over and cut me and Brandon down. He said two words. "You Go."

Seems the French, Italian, Canadian, German, African, American, Russian, Liborators had fought their way through the front lines of the 'Towel-Heads!'

THE CORD

"My arms were tied behind my back. I was blindfolded, but I could tell they were tied behind me with the kind of cord found only on old-fashioned irons."

"Does it make any difference? I'm Doctor Roy Peacock and I am John's Psychiatrist. John O'Rourke had been telling me about a recurring nightmare.

"Yes, Dr. Peacock, it makes a difference because I was going to smash my tormentors in the face it was connected to. The cord is a cloth substance. Round cloth. A faded brown color. Tan and off white, now. He knew his iron cords. He was intimately familiar; with what he was describing.

Dr. Peacock interrupted, "John; how is it you're so familiar with a simple iron cord?"

A shudder came over John O'Rourke. He began to sweat. He opened and closed his fists and began to rock his head back and forth on my therapeutic couch. Eyes blinking open and closed. Dry tongue licking at dry lips.

"Relax; John. Relax."

"My father..." John said. "Mommy, f ... f ... father beat me with one."

"Why John? Why would anyone want to beat anyone with a cord like that?"

"I smashed his face with the iron... His temper was awful after that."

JUICED

"They were put in the back of the eighteen wheelers and the 'juice' was put to them. Night and day. Day and night.

"They were strapped down on the metal gurneys with blood troughs running around them and all sorts of 'nasties' were performed."

I was talking about the people smuggled across the Canadian border: French. Germans. Russians, Polish; Irish; Apolitical and political alike.

I was making a statement to the A.B.P. (American Border Patrol). I work in the A.B.P. undercover. "There were false walls in these trucks. False walls and false ceilings. On the open roads a green light flickered on and off and the grotesqueries began. The torments and tortures stopped in residential areas. The ones who succumbed early were the lucky ones. The back roads of the North Country went on and on for mile after mile....

"And the screaming ... the screaming ... After being 'broken'; a captive was sometimes let go. Who knows? The damn fool may be unlucky enough to run afoul of a 'Randy-Assed Mad Trucker. Men women and children went mad just hearing 'Rubber Slap Asphalt.'

"And the Truck-ers?"

"You want to know from an American Border Patrol Agent about the truckers? 'They're paid cash.' American cash for Flesh Trade..."

HOT DOG

I have mustard, ketchup; salt and pepper. I have hamburgers; hotdogs, macaroni salad and potato salad. I have all this; and I have more than all this. I've got a backyard pool. 20'x30'. Eight feet at the deep end. I've got a flat screen TV. I wheel out in the backyard at my picnics. It's an H.D. TV. High Definition. You never know when you might want to see the dirt under Paul O'Neal's fingernails. We have an easy life these days. I joke about it. We take a cab to get to our car. Four Mercedes Benzes cost less than one Rolls Royce.

There's waste. There's waste and excess. We're soft and spoiled. These are our luxuries. We've worked for them. Sweated blood, sweat, and tears for them to get where we are. Our ancestors worked to rise above others. Our parents worked to be a cut above others; and we do too. Our great grandparents worked themselves to the bone to achieve their success and their great grandparents before them.

We can own a house. A boat. We can live in a mansion; penthouse or cabin. We can do this in the land of liberty. We can do as we wish in the privacy of our own homes. We can't break the law or do things that are unholy; but we're pretty much free to do as we please. Because we won our freedom. We fought and lived and we will die to defend our freedom. And we'll do it forever.

Just don't mess with my stuff. I'll shoot you. Especially your furriers.

THE CAT

"Meow." "Meow." "Meow." All day long. "Meow." "Meow." "Meow." Kitty had long since been put in my subconscious—and kept there. She could claw furniture. Arch her back against my legs for food or water or, in her own inimitable way, make it known her litter box needed emptying by rubbing against the bathroom doorjam. Sound familiar Kitty? Sound familiar?

Oh. What am I beefing about? I can reach the doorknob. Come and go as I want. Pour myself a glass of milk before going to bed.

A cat will roll over and play dead for you for a sweet pet down the back. Kitty knows when I've been with someone. If she could give you a cold shoulder, well then, buddy guess what? You've just landed in Antarctica. Kitty is possessive in the P-O-S-S-E-S-S-I-V-E sense of the word. And she's patient.

Oh kitty is ever so patient. Some night when you're bone-tired and lying on your back dead but to the loudest noises kitty jumps on the bed. On my chest. She passes a fur ball from her mouth—to mine. Don't tell other people. Her logic reads: you are my human—let others find their own....

GHOST FISH

A fish narrow narrow. And down maybe habitually, 100 feet; gets zero or little sunlight. So a thin pale fish may appear ghostly? Yes. A pale fish deprived of sunlight and little thickness on its sides very well may appear ghostly.

100 Feet down? 100 Feet down? How about 300 Feet down, or 400 or 500 feet underwater? Down in Davy Jones's locker. The deep six. I wasn't a sailor so I must ask: Did something of significance happen at six fathoms? The deep six. Or is this where earthbound souls reside? Six feet under? So, anyway; you're ellusive, altruistic, ghost fish? Watch your toes, kids. Watch your little piggies. Some of these heinous-assed fish might nibble off a pinky or two, thinking no more about it than nibbling corn nibblets. And if these are "ghost fish"? Can they invade the bones prior to a nibble, curl it and bite off part of the foot at the same time he goes for the nibblett?

I'll tell ya' won't say nothing. In fact, 'cause as we all know there's ghostly-like catfish, lying low near the muddy bottom of a (lake) body of water. Could it be we think our toes are being eaten off as 'cat' has our tongue?' And when we stop and think about all this, we start laughing uproariously and say nothing?

Thanks a lot, "ghost fish!"

THE BOAT

We were, as people far out to sea say, "taking on water." We weren't far out to sea; we were on a lake and yes the boat was full of water. But then we were full of booze so we simply didn't give a hoot.

"Hey, Mary, Pass me some rum." This was in the style of 'Yo ho ho and a bottle of rum.' But it had me thinking. It's not safe to drink and drive—and it's not safe to boat and drink...

"Guys! Guys!" when I had their attention I began my diatribe. "Twenty years ago when I was in college this guy wrote a short piece called, 'Ghost Fish' we had to critique." Some of the guys said, "So what..." or "Aw; c'mon." But I was relentless.

Besides the girls said, "Quiet. Let him tell the story."

"It's a paradox; and I want to hear your reaction to it when I've finished. In this story; this guy referred to his toes as being the equivalent to nibblets of corn for panfish and how as their toes were getting bitten off all they could do was laugh and laugh again, if not harder when they spoke of this incident to the authorities. Well anyway; I've come to a remembrance of the story again. Maybe, just maybe they'd wandered into a school of 'Ghost Fish'; and [THAT] when they had done so they were blind drunk..."

There was an audible sucking in of breath at this moment. One of the guys said, "That's not funny, Martin."

"Who said I was going to say anything funny, Junior?

Jesus by now we were all in the water (lake), hanging onto the boat. I started to laugh.
"What's so funny?"
"'Ghost fish' can't bite through shoes..."

THE BOAT II

Time was on my side. E.M.T. (Emergency Medical Technician). I showed the kids what to do if a car rolled over. How to remove riders and drivers. Night and day. Spring. Summer. Winter. Fall.
    Trapped in a house on fire. Treat a gunshot wound. I patiently explained to my students what to do in the event of a hurricane, tornado, earthquake, flood. Day and night. Spring. Summer. Winter. Fall.
    In a mining disaster. Lost at sea.
    Taught how to teach. Taught aspiring Emergency Medical Technicians how to teach aspiring Emergency Medical Technicians how to react to a drowning. Heat exhaustion. Lost in the woods.
    But; my thing is to get these kids in a boat on a lake; at night and let Nature take its course. Do no harm; where you can do no good. Hypocratic Oath. They laugh. They cry. Mainly they laugh. If Sue can't ski to rescue someone with a broken leg; she compensates by being the best mountain climber in the class. Yeah, we get out on that boat and we laugh and we cry; but mainly we laugh and we get mad. But mainly we get happy and suddenly in my instructor's voice; "You've graduated. Good luck."

HYDROCHLORIC ACID

The train tanker was sitting on its side just off the track. It even had its top on still. That's why what happened to those 2,000 people didn't bother me. No. Didn't bother me much at all.

I was just playing this God-awful joke. They say you could hear those nosey-bodies bellowing for miles around. Yeah I loosened the track. I loosened the track and I set the fires that would blow toward the train. And I suppose those that weren't quite fast enough to outrun the flames might what? Catch fire? Spur a panic? And yeah, I guess it was me that marked the tanker; 'Water'!!!

It didn't bother me those 2,000 'busy-bodies' 'went-the-way-the-wild-goose-goes' because; I didn't tell them to bring a bunch of pails looking for the 'liquid-gold'. (Oil) I'd said in the newspapers the train would be carrying in the tankers. That's what they get for being greedy! Yeah. I reported in the news there would be water and oil in the tankers in just such an event. An accident.

But wouldn't ya' rather have the skin burn off your body slow-like from the natural fire than dissolve from Hydrochloric Acid burns?

STIFF STUFF

She is a woman. She is a woman; much as the other was. She's dead. She's dead and she's fossilized and she's mine. And she's dead, and she's fossilized and she's mine. She's mine. All mine. And being all mine as mine, she'll loosen up. She'll relax. Her taut exterior will soften and we'll walk. We'll walk and talk and dance.
    We'll walk and I won't walk in front as she may not follow. And I'll not walk behind as she may not lead. We'll walk and talk and dance and be as friends.
    I tell Margaret alarming things she's nonplussed at, shocking events. She lets it go in one ear and out the other. We bathe. We rest. We eat. And we love. We love. Of course we love. It would be unnatural, not to love.
    And sometimes our love is a hard love that an observer can't or won't understand. And as often as not, our love is a soft yearning love. So we keep our love secret. We keep our love secret and we keep other parts of ourselves secret. And we keep our secrets for long and short times.
    Margaret and I like winter. Winter is our nighttime. We can pull the blinds and curtains with none of us the wiser. We do for each other in the winter for long periods of time.
    That's how we are. That's the way we are, and that's the way we'll stay—until death do us part.
    But we'll do what we do side by side and be as friends.

SHOW OFF

I think of "work-ethic" when I think of dis-honesty. Non-existent, in a word. Honesty.

People work ceaselessly to get a little money, that is, more, inbound-missive; than having anything to do with a fatter wallet. Paid $20.00 an hour in a supervisory position, will an executive bend down and pick a scrap of paper off the floor; or will he have what he refers to as a low-life subordinate kneel at his boot? Duh. One must show superiority at all cost. Quash the bugs. So what's the count? A superior superior? My superioration is bigger than your superioration! Bite me.

Oh volunteer do you swear to be and at all times and in all manner to perform and deny all help and be a slop bucket? Take a ticket and wait your turn!

Do you swear to destroy, help pardon, assist, love, life? Raise your left hand. Place your right hand on the 'Blue-Book' and grovel!

Ahh, they say. It's a beef and moan session. A hissy fit! No; it's a reality check! I wrote the book on having been a *pound downed pissant*. I wrote the book on that and it shot to the top of the best seller list for twenty years. And I wrote twenty more bestselling; 'Beat Down the Bottom books that stayed up on top of the 'charts'!

And I'm a star. And it's lonely at the top. And it makes ya' mean. Mean. Stay out of my way. Keep a healthy distance between us. Don't 'eyeball' me! Jump when I say jump; and don't come back down 'til I've told 'ya to! BE THE BUG!

MAGIC

Money is Magic. I spell magic like that, not majic 'cause when 'ya got it, 'ya got it! And when 'ya got it, 'ya feel like a million bucks! But majic for me has a significance. I'll soon tell you why. Magic is the proper spelling of the word, but the significance of spelling ma-gic majic for me is as follows:
Yeah. Money has a feel good feeling attached; variable with the increase or diminishment associated with it. Now you're probably at this point saying to yourself, "Cut to the chase dammit!" I tell those that listen in this 'rubber-room,' the money spoke to me. Ya feel like a million bucks; and it's really majic how that works, but it'd make a Pharaoh roll over in his tomb knowing the wealth of the kingdom; just now!

Stodgy money! Old New York money! Boston wealth! Chicago cash! It's a majic thing looking down from their lofty heights, high places! Eating steak and drinking champagne and not seeing the dirt poor refund a nickel soda can. It's majic!

And I say, would some dirt poor soul sell out the Lord for forty pieces of silver? No, I think not.

I do think, however, it's within the realm of possibilities; that if the Lord returned, some wealthy sicko might take forty pieces of silver—and maybe claim a poor soul did it. It's a matter of semantics.

It's MAJIC!

THE TABLE

The yellowing dog-eared tabloid lay on the table where I'd thrown it yesterday. On page 8 was the story I wanted and had cut out. "Martians Over Swamp." That's all. I had dug through dirty, crusty, crumbling, tabloids just to get that story. Martians over Swamp. Not a swamp in Mississippi. Not a swamp in Florida. My swamp in Tennessee. Great Neck Swamp. The Martians had hovered over my Great Neck Swamp in Tennessee thirty years ago and had abducted me. And ya know how I know?

Ya know how someone claims they were abducted but can't remember the spaceship or what color the Martians were? Green or yellow? Well I got a souvenir. I must have done something right because smack dab in the middle of my living room is a table. Maybe it's better to call it a block. It's heavy. I never moved it and those government types couldn't move it either. There's no point in trying to eat off it, either. It's square; and it's solid. There's something else about my table. There are hieroglyphics on all five sides. I almost have the puzzle solved.

I'm reasonably sure it starts out like the song (Nothing from nothing leaves nothing—" "You gotta have something if you want to be with me ... Now let me quickly guess the rest of this: On July 7th we will pick up the owner of the house within which we've placed the table...

Oh, God ... It's July 6th...

ONE ON ONE

Basketball will set you straight if you have a little too much energy. Adrenalin. Badminton; golf; table tennis; ping pong; pin ball, pool, bowling. Friendly pastimes. Happy fun.
It's when your opponent pokes out your eye with his cuestick. Because he's been doing Meth. 'Cause he got mad! It's when your bowling partner throws a bowling ball at your head; because he's had one too many shots of scotch! That's not sport. Competition; that's aggression! When Igor, Ivan, or Vladd attacks you with a claw hammer and you have a claw hammer to defend yourself with for sport, you better leave a mark. You better you better you bet!
Redemption is a swing away. I hope you're packing steroids, beta blockers, pain killers. And No-Doze. Don't forget the No-Doze. Of course the double-ring of Dobermans smelling, almost tasting the blood and gore, will keep you focused with the growling, snapping, barking cacophony. And the taunting of the fans. Yeah; the bloodlust. The blood-curdling screams of fans needing mayhem, bloodshed, carnage.
The Roman gladiators never saw as much blunt force trauma; broken torso rendered limbless!
These wounds endure. These screams and shrieks will be heard in the thirtieth century.
Yeah, one on one is fun. One on one in the circle of death isn't fun. They say leave your troubles behind. Have a good time. They also say I hope I have a cyanide capsule ready

to bite down on, implanted in a tooth and that I don't leave home without it...
 Aheh; Aheh; Aheh.

DOWNLOADED

I had, 'hit the fan' as they say in French. Agghhh. So what? I was tired and if I thought about it long enough (why I had 'hit the fan'), I could justify it to myself. Tired. Yes. Downbeaten. Dead tired. The police officer is taking this statement: I was in jail when it went down. I broke the rules and regulations of the jail. I cut this joker from his right side to his left side with a homemade shiv. And you wanna know why. I wrote the rules and regulations of this crummy joint.

I'd been in the army blowing the crap out of gooks and some no account had put my sister on the streets. Well things like that fester in you. I popped that pimp. Clear as a whistle. I admit it, I killed 'im: but what I don't get is this psycho bullshit I'd been told not to talk to her about the good tricks or killin' gooks or nothin . . . Then this Holy Roller comes along..."Come clean. Come clean."

"Hallelujah"...

I had even gone so far as to cut off knifin' these bad men. But they kept at me. They kept at me. Enlighten us, I was told. Write it down. The knifings. The tricks. See if ya' don't get an extra biscuit if you're good. Jesus! What were they thinking??? Live it up, Jonesey. Cut some people in here.

"What? In the joint?"

But anyway seems these 'hardened' folk like the gory details. Cut a con left to right under his belly button that mother will spill 'is guts. Same thing—right to left. Sometimes they let out a yelp; sometimes they let out a grunt. A holler! Let it out. Write it down. The cons had me over a barrel. Tell us the sound of their guts splashin' on the floor. What it looked like. Did they soil themselves?

Ohhh; how much of this can I take? How can I live with myself? I'm caught between a rock and a hard place. Kill and learn to dig it; or be killed and forget about worrying about it. Things got tense. A sergeant I'd served with in the army got put in the joint here with me.

Okay I thought. Be aloof. Be cool. Don't let on you're a killer among killers. Then and only then, I found the reason he was brought in. Seems he put a bat to use on pimp killers....

FILL

I'd about had my fill. The guy upstairs was cutting the zero slack. Zilch! It was okay though; I was gonna like the guys at the plant say, pour a cauldron of slag up his ass! I work at the steel mill, needless to say. I had it figured. Coat 'im like a bell. Ring his chimes over and over.

Sleep deprivation was about to take on a new definition. Can you hear me now? Funtime. Me and my little crass antics of encasing this nutball in metal; I worked out with my own personal Skel-Bots. They never did know they weren't to harm someone and that they were harming someone—and they never will—not from me. So I got the screwball I couldn't make understand walk quietly encased in metal. Swinging from chains in my living room. And doesn't he put in long sleep-deprived years?

Yes; the screwball from upstairs who didn't listen to me about walking quietly in the apartment above me, swinging in my living room, encased in metal, put in long years.

I tell myself he's lucky. I tell myself if he'd been in the Human/Skeleton wars back in '08 and had pulled this bullshit he'd been put to a firing squad. So I guesstimate it's like twenty? Twenty-three years since nutball started hanging around (I had a hole for him to eat; a colostomy insertion; and; a urinary tube) and people started to notice a big swelling in my right upper arm. No it's true enough; when I'm watching a baseball game or, working on my computer, I 'Gong' screwball with my right upper arm because I'm right-handed. And because the guy from upstairs took swing after swing as a bell—my muscle grew. And when the authorities investigated? Horrified at my ingenuity, aghast, they cut off my arm. You may ask, Do you care? No I care not. The authorities were aghast and horrified at my ingenuity, and cut off my arm; but they were stepping over the line when they took my little brass ball-peien hammer!

THE HEART

A sailor in advanced boot camp is to free dive 100 feet; A marine is to remove his mask in the gas chamber and shout out his name, rank, and serial number. An Air Force Cadet is to be in a simulated 3G's Pull Out; a soldier in this Man's Army is to take a shot of Epinephrine to the heart. It seems scandalous to do this to our men and women; but, as the song says, "It's all in the game..."

But again. Moe Sanchez has a problem. He joined the army back in '72. As we all know, it's 2035. Moe Sanchez is 83 years old. He joined when he was twenty. Moe Sanchez is the world's oldest living 'active' private. He couldn't, wouldn't take the shot in the heart. Way back when Moe Sanchez had been told he had a heart murmur. The call to arms is a strong call indeed. Naught will prevent us from signing on the dotted line. Thing is; Moe Sanchez didn't realize what the Army, Navy, Mar-ines, Air Force, required for advancement. Ahyup ... Moe Sanchez had a bit of a problem....

THE CASE

This is a continuing Journal Entry. The year is 2040. As we all know, three years ago I captured the Serial Killer known as the Hooker. By all accounts, there were fourteen typos in the papers.

The Hookers Hook was a meat hook—just to *set* the record straight. The eight detectives in the neighborhood were my bothers. In four years I'll be a detective on the Chicago Police Force like my brothers and my dad. It won't be hard.

I want to take down the pervs and perps. I've got meat on me now. I was skin and bones when I was 'hooker-bait'. I see myself in a confrontation with a militant or radical and know what I would do. A knee to the groin will cause a grown man to crumple to the ground gasping for air. Grabbed from the front by an assailant in bear-hugs, a sharp blow to the ears, causes sudden release.

Yes I'll join the Chicago Police Force, and if all goes well I'll make Detective. But in the meantime; I'll join the Federal Bureau of Investigation. A three-year stint in the Federal Bureau of Investigation.

CYCLE

Plank Monroe pushed out his kickstand with his right foot; and let his bike rest on it. Things were fuzzy around the peripherals. Sometimes things got fuzzy. More and more—lately. He took off his helmet and stood up. His handlebars were tilted away so the right one was pointed upward. Plank put his helmet on that one.

First it was the kid today. He was in front of an A&P supermarket and this kid says; "Does it back up." Plank barely looked at the kid. "Sure." An old man said; "Hmph." "Take this quarter and get some candy." He gave Plank a scathing look.

Then it was some girl. "You have a permanent convertible." "Yeah" Plank said, "Not real warm in the winter." The girl smiled, and Plank grimaced.

But it was the cop. It was; 'Officer Friendly' Sergeant Muldoon. Plank was cruising 55 miles an hour thinking nothing more than going over to Freddy's and chugging a couple of cold Buds. The sirens and flashing red and blue halogen lights in his rearview mirror blew him out of his reverie. His first thought was to throttle up and book. He felt his gall rise. Shit. "Chuck-you Farley," Plank said when the cop came up to him.

"Keep your hands on the handlebars, after you give me your license." The cop had mirror sunglasses and razor thin lips that didn't frown, smile, or move when he spoke.

Plank couldn't read this guy and was suddenly spooked.

"What the hell is this all about? Is it a bust?" Stoney said nothing. Plank worried. Sometimes the man came down hard on bikers; not calling it harassment which five from out of five guys knew it was, but armed robbery I suspect, or going 85 in a residential area.

"Talk when you're told to, freak."

Shit. "Hey..." Mace and a nightstick hit Plank at the same time. "Shut-Up!" Plank sat on his bike; but his legs had begun to shake. His eyes burned and tears spilled out. He breathed through his open mouth, suddenly felt nauseated.

The cop reached into his shirt pocket and Plank flinched. "What do you see here, freak?" The cop held out pictures of motorcycles that had gone through various stages of mayhem. There were sheets with blood smears over lumps in the roads too. Plank didn't like where this was going.

"Accidents?"

"Right, freak. Accidents."

"With eighteen wheelers? Cabs?"

"Yes, freak we see that. At this point the cop paused for effect. "We see motorcycles!"

"What's this got to do with me?"

"Well I'll tell ya' freak. These 'bikers'—and trust me there's a fair share of gals who thought they could drink and ride. Maybe smoke some grass. Maybe some of them didn't want to wear a helmet. Queer. Makes me look like a fairy. Problem is, if they get used to wearing a helmet each and every time, or not revving your bike in front of an old age home, over and over, or breaking any other law, when a biker DOES wear a helmet maybe doesn't think of the pictures I just showed you and ralph in their helmet and wipe out..."

THE QUITTEST

When I first tell people what happened, they get big in the eyes, their mouths drop open, and I'm looked at askance.
I quit smoking.
I quit drinking.
I quit gambling.
I quit cursing.
I quit sexual activity.
I had nothing to do with these sudden changes. It's God's doing, and I beg for the mercy to accept these blessings. A lot of people getting help pass away. They get help too late. A lot of people who don't get treatment die. Some people linger. They suffer. It isn't easy for them. They use the last resort.
I'm trying to quit quitting. I've been noticing I've been trying to hold my breath for longer and longer periods of time. I think I'm trying to quit breathing. Things have gone way too far. I think I'm thinking; I'm trying to quit my circulatory system. Quit circulatory-ing.
I'm in a void. No; a vacuum. I'm in a flux all the time. Quit. Quit. Quit. All the time. I don't want to quit alpha one. Living. I want to be going at life 360 degrees; and digging it. More. And more. And more.
But now I'm in another strangeness. Have to stop digging life without 'habits' because for all intents and purposes I'm sappin' the life right out of ya's. I 'saw' things. I 'saw' I was connected to all other life by ethereal imbilical cords. Much as an octopus with its lovin' arms wrapped around a

too-near and careless dolphin. I'm caught between nuts and crazy. The leeches of the sea—squid and octopuses. And can you say what will repel a leech? Salt. And is or is not sea water chock full of saline??? AAAUUUUHHHH…

THE TEAM

"A chain is as strong as its weakest link." "First one on last one off." "Last one on first one off." "One thin dime." "Show the little lady you're a big spender, mister."

I was getting what they called in 'Nam a 'rush,' 'free association.'

These thoughts and a dozen like them were clamoring around in my skull for attention. I was crazy cool. We were in the coffee shop sucking up 'high octane'. Debby was smart. Tailored black hair, short, pixie cut. White blouse. Thin, not sheer. Plaid skirt.

"Earth to Bobby." We teased each other. "Bowling Saturday?"

"Yeah, Hon."

"Bobby? What's wrong?"

"I can't focus, Debby. I flip out."

"You have to slow down. You're going to give yourself a heart attack."

We looked at each other. Debby's right. I'm burning out. I'm running around like a chicken with its head cut off.

"Hey Bobby, maybe a doctor can help you."

"Debby, that's not an option."

"Okay. No doctor. We could go to an Island."

I don't know if she is kidding or serious but that was the most romantic thing anyone had suggested in years. "You know babe, you're right. I'd love to chase you around beaches in a bikini." She laughed.

"Are you serious?"

"Yeah, hon. The whole nine yards. Buy an Island. A boat. I've got family money stashed away. And we could be cozy."

We both ordered a cappuccino. We had to make plans.

CONFUSION REIGNS

There was a time when I was much more clear-headed. I had lofty goals. Keen vision. I was going to name cities. Streets. None of that will come to pass now. Yeah, I wrote four books.
 I wrote four books but half the generation I grew up with thinks music rules. That movie shows are to be copied for real life. God help the generations after the one I grew up in.
 Or this one!
 Four books. My claim to fame. They're not even close to being on the best seller list. Idle money. I spent idle cash for a chance at the brass ring. I became frail and angry at the lack of recognition. But along with anger and a lack of cash came love. A love of writing that is never ending. I'll write ten more books. One hundred more. Yeah, I changed. I used to grovel. Beg. I've got dignity now. I prayed to stop begging and I did. I stopped sniveling.
 But, I say all this as a kind of warning. I got proud and bold but maybe, just maybe, not quite so advantageously for my enemies. For people I don't like. People who make demands on others. Maybe like real and/or imagined demands were made on me? Maybe this is nonsense. I was meek. I was a bookworm. Like the title of this short piece suggests, maybe if I go straight to hell, I'll be able to call a shot or two!

THE UNDOING

Me and Pa never knew what would happen or why we did what we did, but I'm glad we did it. It wouldn't make any difference anyway. We LIKE to do what we do. Ma died a few years back. Me and Pa buried her out in back of the house; in the pumpkin patch. She would've liked that. She was part of the 'undoing'.

Let me tell ya' right off, Ma got buried deep but didn't some big pumpkins grow by her? Back to the undoing. Me, Pa, and Ma lived on a farm and these green city kids used to come around and gawk at us. Hit our mailbox with a baseball bat. Go in our pumpkin patch and smash 'em. So we grew corn.

We grew 100 acres of corn and we grew 100 acres of pumpkins. And let me tell you something—we had those Undoing Parties at Halloween!

We had Mazes in the corn rows. We served these green city kids spiked cider and spiked pumpkin pies. At first we didn't mean to go 'Hog Wild' on these punks. Me, Ma, and Pa. We thought the stuff we spiked the punch and pies with was ordinary rat poison. It was a lot worse than that. P.C.P. and L.S.D. We just thought these kids were gullible.

A glass tub. "Okay everybody, line up. We're going to bob for pumpkins!" I swear there was an electric twitter throughout the crowds, every year! But they 'bobbed' for pumpkins. They ralphed in the water and me and Pa cleaned it.

They drowned themselves and me and Pa dragged 'em

off for burial later: good fertilizer; for both corn, and pumpkins.

And they shat themselves. Both me and Ma laughed at that. Once in a while there was a variety to the proceedings. A Rube would balance on a barrel with a noose around his/her neck, and try to take a bite from the apple dangling just out of reach. It didn't matter; their hands were tied behind their backs. And laugh? God how they would laugh! I got to the point where I couldn't wait for the laughing to stop.

Maybe tilt the barrel a little?

THE RAID

Check this out. I was away from home one fall for about a week. It was cold, wet and miserable. Needless to say, I was out on the streets in a strange city! But I didn't use. No no, no. Drinking was the big thing. I drank like a fish. But I had no money. Lots of pride and no money. It was a moot point if I wanted a drink or not.

So I figured I'd walk home. Five miles? A cinch. Ten miles? No big deal. Then—a couple of cops picked me up. Where are you headed? Blankety-Blank.

I got home and pulled the covers up, but the next morning, tapping on the door. "Who's there?" "It's me, Marilyn. Where have you been?" I know it's Saturday. Marilyn is a case manager at a famous hospital. Case managers don't work at famous hospitals on Saturdays.

She came in and sat and I talked. I talked like a canary. I was scared, sick and frustrated. I felt like I was being set up. "Marilyn, did you call the cops? I have a healthy aversion to authority," "No, Craige. I love you and Jesus loves you." I missed a signal. On one pretext or another, Marilyn stepped outside. There was thunderous banging on my door. "Police, Open up!" I could see them out in front and out in back. A S.W.A.T. team.

I grabbed a knife and began to hack at myself. Throat, neck. I remember pushing the knife up into the soft part of my neck in the back. Up inside my brain?

A couple of years later, I wrote a book about this and that I don't smoke any more. I don't drink anymore.

Problem is I can't come near myself with a razor. I can't shave—even electric razors make me cringe!!! I get, "Watch what you pray for" a lot!

THE SCREW

I got shot. I got shot by an arrow and I didn't like it. I got shot by an arrow twice. A deer arrow has a Razor Head. Ooooh. I got shot in the right gluteus maximus—rear end—and it traveled through my left hip bone and out. I then got shot by a second arrow—Broad-Head that almost severed my carotid artery. Why? Why? For a prank—that's why.

The guys and I got together thinking, wouldn't it be a slam wearing deer-colored clothes out on the hills and roads we lived on. Some slam. I could hear somebody shrieking and I lost sight of my friends. It was me who was shrieking and I blanked out when I was first pierced. It was when I came to that my neck felt like it was in a vice.

My buddies were holding themselves in various spots bemoaning their lot in life. It was kind of funny; really; four guys yelling and puking; and bleeding all over the place.

I looked around. Two guys in hunting toga were coming in a trail out of the woods perpendicular to the road. Jesus. They were laughing and acting all the while; they hadn't just handicapped four guys for life. Fuck. Look, Louie, two arrows in that one. Calm down, Carmen. You'll scare away other game. Game? Game?

Louie and Carmen took up a conversation. Sometimes they had to shout to be heard above the shrieking. Ya know what, Louie? What, Carmen? These guys go out in the woods, see. Yeah, yeah. And they see something rustle the bushes, so they shoot and it's a guy. So the one guy tells the other one to run back to town and get help. Well, Doc struggles up the hill and makes the pronunciation. "He would'a lived if ya hadn'ta gutted 'im!"

Jesus-ker-crimminy!! I'm dying. We're dying and Carmen and Louie are cracking wise!!! Say it ain't so, Joe. They wandered off and a self-described; randy-assed trucker came and radioed our position to the authorities.

I've often wondered if they knew about the one; "There was this deer with a slow gait . . .

ROAD RUMPS

The car on the left, a blue Punch-Bug, passed us again. Punch-Bug, no punch back. Gary was driving. Gary always drives. It's his blue/green Mercury. He gleefully slugs me as the Punch-Bug passes and slows. Slows and passes. I grit my teeth and grimace. I have the leisure to look over into Punch-Bug. It unnerves me. A man and woman are hitting on each other over there. Older people. She hits him and says something; he drives with one hand a moment, hits her and says something, and returns his hand to the wheel. This is a signal to her to hit him again. What are they saying? Not two outs, man on first... No. No. No. More like Punch-Bug. No punch back. So I'm watching the road for Gary from the shot-gun position; and watching and thinking about the blows and verbal advice each is giving the other in the car over and I say, "Gary, blow your horn!" "Huh? What the hell have you been smoking there, Reeves, bug?" "No I'm serious, Gary. Lay on the horn before they're black and blue," I said jerking my thumb at the Punch-Bug over the way ...

Well; Gary took this 70 m.p.h. stretch of road to go hysterical. He started laughing. He was laughing so hard he was grabbing at himself so he wouldn't wet. Choking, gasping, grabbing, laughing, wiping tears. Gary was in quite a state. We were on cruise-control as I knew, because every time we hit the highway to a ball game (baseball, football) we went cruise-control; so I grabbed the wheel and gently steered the car to the shoulder of the road. Gary gently touched the brakes. But what I want to know will there always be something hysterical to make me out to be the hero?

THE REMINDER

First of all there was a post-it on my desk about the Fourth of July picnic. There were six of us going: John and Mary Turner, Bill Harmony, Sue Wilcox, Larry Younger and me, Alexander Sanchez. The other guys don't know I'm Russian. I wonder if it makes any difference. Later; but still a day or two before the Fourth; there were three messages on my answering machine: Two from Sue Wilcox; and one from Bill Harmon. We're climbing the corporate ladder. We're at various levels but close enough in longevity in Harper, Harper and Smith, Insurance, to have a Fourth of July picnic at Hampton Beach, Florida. We work in Miami.

Somehow I was going to have to cancel the picnic. Not just for me, for all of us. I had overcome a communiqué [that] Russian K.G.B. agents were going to 'dispatch' Mary Turner. She was found unsuitable for her husband of thirty years, John Turner. I know some people at the newspaper who would make things seem that John went North to be with his family after Mary mysteriously dropped dead; but what on earth was I going to do about the Fourth of July? It rained on the 4th; 5th; and 6th; and every time it rains tears well up in my eyes.

THE DRILL

I saw it but I couldn't believe it. Haroldeson had picked up a pneumatic drill with one hand and tossed it thirty feet. The thing weighs 80 pounds. Yeah. Haroldeson was mad. A driver had come racing by the construction site where we were working on the road and that unlucky driver had hit a puddle next to Harvey Haroldeson—drenching him.

I say unlucky driver because the hurtled pneumatic drill, thrown as a spear, struck the driver—still racing up the street—between the shoulder blades. He had subsequently been half turned in his seat giving Haroldeson the bird, so that left a mark. Then; Haroldeson grabbed two bags of cement (one under each arm, thank you very much), began whistling and went back to work.

That's when I took up psychology. Under what circumstances will a road crew push its people to throw drills thirty feet at people and begin whistling with a bag of cement under each arm, while returning to work like nothing happened? Huh? The cops came. The situation was explained. A wise guy cop said, "What? You didn't dump the cement on 'im?" I like that cop's sense of humor.

There was a guy fresh out of army bootcamp, skull still red and sore from the scalping of his hair, like all the other recruits that have to be processed quickly, who dug drill. He was sent to me as recruits notoriously loathe for close order drill. "I like the discipline, John." I let him call me by my first name. We had a one in a million with this guy. "I like the structure, discipline, and fraternity-like resemblance of the army. Oh God, what are we doing to our youth?

The last I heard; he was drilling troops in a back-water country—in case of 'disturbance.' "The alarm blare, you keep out of the way, and make beds; sweep and mop the floors, make lunch ... That's what they told me when I got the job." This was Bill Meadows. He had just gotten a volunteer job at the local fire station. "They said, 'You know the drill.' I forgot I left a cigarette burning!"

THE DRILL II

First off, I'm a dentist. Second, you just aren't going to believe me. I was in the office the other day. Boy was I in the office. I was working on Suzie R—C—'s—teeth and suddenly; I wasn't.

You see; I was drilling and I needed to adjust the suction. I had told Suzie, if you need me to stop, raise a hand. Well that's not the point. I had the drill in my right hand, and I switched it over to my left hand and reached into Suzie's mouth with my right hand to do just that; adjust the suction.

Well, I'm right-handed, so, so far—so good. But my right leg jerked at that moment. My right foot was on the pedal that controls the drill. Well, Suzie hears the drill and bites two fingers off my right hand. That's not all. I yelled and drove the whirring drill into my left leg. That's not all, either.

The fabric of my pants wound around the drill, burning into my kneecap. And it gets hot. All of a sudden I see smoke puffing out of my knee, so I squirt a little water on the hole in my left kneecap, and I get a shock. At least I had the presence of mind to tell Suzie to spit.

But it was the next weekend, and I'm not making this up—Thankee Jesus—I was driving in the south west. Arizona. Texas. Utah. Let's go back to Texas a minute. I was watching people drilling an oil rig. I really don't know what that drill bit hit, but it came up outa that ground like a missle. Problem is (and I still don't know why he did it), a guy directly under the falling drill, threw himself on his back, under it.

Well a couple folk puked as this guy is screaming his fool head off, and whirling around and around from the force of the still twirling drill bit stuck on him, and some of these guys are; laughing fit ta burst.

Some other strange stuff went on lately, too. I see these science-fiction shows. I'm not saying I give them an ounce of credence, but let's just say ... I have brain damage—head injuries. In some cases serious. I remember once I was drunk and I got in a bar fight. I got knocked ass-over-tea-kettle down some cement stairs.

When I got to the hospital, big macho me says, "I don't need any anesthesia." Well mister tough guy; if you don't need any anesthesia; maybe the doctor don't need no schooling ... But anyway; every once in a while, I'll think maybe I got a lobotomy. Back brain lobotomy. Drill up any good memories???

MURPHY REGINALD

Murphy Reginald leaned into the shovel again, this time scooping up slushy wet snow and moist dirt, muttering under his breath about the fact that that nitwit Slim Jim was doing nothing, more than doing nothing—not here—than most anywhere.

Murphy did a quick re-con. Headstones pale-bottom teeth pointing upward to a dissimilar sky. Cloudy and bleak with a low big moon covered mostly in cloud. Trees of foliage on their branches. Elongated shadow cast by mausoleum and wormy mounds of earth. Discerting wind howling out of the north. Nothing blocking its westward travels. Dogs barking to chase night madness away. Murphy Reginald spit.

Slim Jim came poking along the cement path to the gravesite Murphy was working. "Where the hell have you been?" Murphy was terse.

Slim Jim looked down at his feet. "I found a car."

"I don't give good goddamn rat's ass about you lifting a car when we have a job to do." Murphy kept most of the anger out of his voice and low enough so no one in the vicinity could hear them. Besides once they had the goods; they'd need the car.

"Alright, grab that shovel and make it sing." Murphy couldn't stay mad at Slim Jim long. Slim Jim was a nitwit—but he was Murphy's nitwit. And he was strong. In the wiry sense. They worked about forty minutes until there was an audible 'clunk' of metal hitting wood, both silent, both with much labored breathing. Plumes of white breath were now showing in the moonlit night.

"Get out," Murphy told Slim Jim. "Hand me the ropes."

Slim Jim handed the ropes down to Murphy who put one on one end of the casket and the other rope on the other end of the casket, both ropes equally in the center of the ropes around the coffin, and climbed out of the rave. Together, they then pulled the coffin up, and slid it to one side. It was a fresh body. Cause of death? Drowning. The mortician had restored a pink life-glow shade to the body. And he wanted a dead person. This girl would do. Enter Murphy and Slim Jim. The night-crowd fringe.

What service would you have me perform? The fee is $5,000. You forget this phone number. My alias. The drop for the money. I don't; know what you want with what I provide; just make sure I'm not involved if you're caught. I'll hunt you down like a rabid wolf and tear you a new asshole. A few days later, Murphy and Slim Jim were having a cappuccino at an outdoor café and the stiff walked by smiling and whistling, and they shuddered. Walking with the girl was the mortician; and he was saying to the girl; "You're sure you have no siblings or parents or twins?" And the girl shaking her head laughing and saying; "No Dr. Mortimore, silly. You know what happened to them...."

COMPENDIUM

George Weisblott blew a fart, spat, and scratched his brow. George Weisblott was not an easy man to like. (That was for sure.) "You say you want ten bucks for this bucket O'rust?"

I didn't point out to old George that bucket O'bolts might've been better as old George Weisblott—'might' a said.

I was patient. The Blue Book offer was $3,000. "Yeah, George," I said. "That's my final, offer."

"Okay then," George said and stuck out a grimy hand to seal the deal, "We have a consensus." I could have choked. Where did George come up with; 'consensus'?

I handed George Weisblott a $10,000.00 bill and held out my hand for my change. George Weisblott is my brother, he had borrowed my car to take my girl to the prom and had sequentially wrecked it!!!

CONSPICUOUS

"Keep a low profile, Jervous." When Graudon's Bugs was in a good mood he spoke with a grin. Ordinarily Gary would've used the full non-tendre Jervous and Nerky. He didn't mean to keep a low profile, anyway. He meant don't be conspicuous. But I was. I was conspicuous.

I had cotton pants on. Blue cotton pants with bright yellow stripes running up and down them. Down and up them. And a shirt. I had moccasins on. But I had on a florescent shit. A *PURPLE* florescent shirt. And 'ya know what I couldn't understand? How do you make a shirt florescent?

Me and Bud were going to school tonight, and he said, "Don't be conspicuous, Jervous." But our instructor has a Rottweiler, a big, mean, black-and-brown Rottweiler that likes me in bright clothes. High-profile clothes. High-profile clothes like blue cotton pants with bright, yellow stripes running up and down them. Down and up them. And a *PURPLE* florescent shirt that I couldn't figure out how they made florescent.

BATTY

4 April 2006
Re: Mark Burgess
Pos: Keeper of Bats
Cond.: Deteriorating

Mark Burgess is listless. He can barely stay awake. I bring him into my office and say his name sharply if he begins to doze off. I give him a mild tranquilizer, when he's in my office. He doesn't know it. He thinks he's drinking coffee sans tranquilizer. I'm Dr. Henry Morris. These are ongoing tortures for Mark Burgess, at my discretion.

The appointments in my office are after the staff have gone. I take three tubes of blood in the morning before anyone arrives ... three tubes of Mark Burgess's blood. And then I give him a sleeping pill. Every morning. He says nothing.

He knows it could be worse.

He let my bats out. He let 1,000 of my genetically engineered bats escape their cages. And now he must suffer.

Mark Burgess has told me what he thinks. He can hardly do otherwise. He's tired to the point of dementia. Drugged. Scared beyond reason. He knows the bats sense his weaknesses. The fear. Exhaustion. Not knowing when the next accident will free them and zap—him ... The bats are in cages in a chamber beyond which lie the offices and the main chamber.

I've gotten possession of Mark Burgess's notes; and yes,

the stakes did go up. Mark is made to live within the inner chamber. Should I drug his food...?

c.c.g.
BAT LAB
7731
Ph.D. Henry Morris

SNAKES I

Snakes ran the Serpentine Play. Snakes always ran the Serpentine Play: Tuck the 'Pig-Skin,' dart left, right, left, right, right. Or, whatever seemed evasive to Snakes. Left, left, right, left, left, right.

Usually the defense just called, "On snakes" in their huddles. Snakes, on average gained twenty-seven yards. Twenty-seven yards to Snakes is twenty-seven yards. But there were people watching Snakes. People in black suits and pointy-pointy shoes you could step on cockroaches in corners with. These people's fingers were covered in diamonds too.

Well, seems Snakes got strung up over a tree chipper by the underarms, by chains, because he fell behind in his payments to the boys in the pointy-pointy shoes and black suits.

Seems these guys advised Snakes to; Serpentine out of THIS...

SNAKES II

Snakes ate the pigskin. Pork rind. Pork hocks. Hell. He ate the whole damn pig. We all did.

We were working ambushes and patrols off Highway 101—South Vietnam—thank you very much. We were working ambushes and patrols and when we got a body count, we had a pig roast. We knew 'Snakes' rep, too. Serpentine. Dart left, left. Left, right, left. Worldwide. In the States. Playing football. Twenty-seven yards average. Over here, South Vietnam, Snakes, worked the jungle. Three clicks to and fro. Fro and to. Left, right, left. Serpentining.

Three feet = one meter. One thousand meters = one click. Three clicks = Snakes. Thirty equal = thirty miles = three clicks; roughly speaking. Snake's average three = three clicks. Every day. Every night.

I once heard Snakes stabbed a leech on his chest to eat it from the tip of his K-Bar. I'm not going to ask him though. He might take that personal.

SNAKES III

Snakes had gone north from what my 'ear-to-the-ground' said. Working a lumber camp in the Yukon. Frick! It was February, and the closest I wanted to get to that frigid permafrost was the distance between my heated sleeper, and the tracks that carried it.

We were going to 'watch one another's back.' I'd checked Murphy, Jones, Slick, Fat-Boy. They were doing fine. Reeves and Mulroy were 'good to go' like the taco.

I couldn't figure Snakes up north. Ya' went where ya'd do the most good. What the hell good was the Yukon? I'm Eagle. I'm not a Colonel. I got that name from my C.B., from before the war.

I was dozing in the sleeping car during the seemingly perpetual four-month night and I remembered the teeth! Gold teeth! We had the molar to the left of our left canine tooth emblazoned with an ebony snake surrounded by gold! Mike; 2;1 Give the recognition a signal. Grin. A quick smirk in the bush gave your men our local too.

Snakes wasn't mining gold to return to Vietnam. No. No. Please no....

SNAKES IV

We'd reached Yukon North and went ahead and settled in. I'm still Eagle and this is still the (historical) tale of the 'Mike' Boys out of 'Nam. Snakes was glad to see us. When we'd hit the shit in 'Nam we also carried what was known in military jargon as, Bloopers. M-79's. 'M'-Seven Niner's. Bloopers for short. A medium range hotel-echo (high-explosive) weapon, that could also throw a flare (Illumination) and Willie-Peter (White-Phosphorous). The round(s) for this weapon we carried like our own weapons. The only reason I mention this; is because; we were mobile-and Good to Go. We carried 'Claymores' (Anti-personnel-mines). We smuggled a lot of this 'equipment' through customs. Sure, in the wrong hands—deadly. In our hands? Democracy assured.

We couldn't have run thirty miles and hope to have a slim chance to none to fight to live or die, asking no and sparing no quarter if we hadn't been trained. Training consisted of: hundreds of thousands of pushups. Side straddle hops—many, many, many of them. Close order drill. Countless hours of it. Forced marches. Hour after agonizing hour of it. Running mile after mile. Where endorphins created adrenalin; and adrenalin created muscle; and muscle compounded muscle.

So could we work a gold mine? Does a bear shit in the woods? We could string concertina wire around the gold mines' perimeters and patrol them easily. Easily. This; again in military jargon was 'Skate Duty.'

SNAKES V

I'm Eagle, although not a Colonel, and this is the continuing story of Mike 2;—the boys out of 'Nam 50 years ago. It seems like yesterday. We didn't sneak weapons across customs to war, we bought weapons back to it, in the event ... in the event....

We might have a total conversation in code: A.S.A.P. As soon as possible. F.U.B.A.R. Fucked up beyond all recognition.

A few Vietnamese words thrown in for good measure: Lai Di Nook—bring me water. Di Di Moi—beat it. Mainly we used these codes to call in Fire Missions or Air Strikes or some such.

Alpha, Bravo, Charley, Delta, Echo ... or some such wordage; Depending on branch of service: marines army, navy, air force.

Now we were moving north again. Snakes sold Roger Slaughter Gold Mining. He cashed in on millions sent to Swiss Bank accounts. I'm really, really sure he put Mike 2:1 Squad Members: Slick, Fatboy, Murphy, Jones, Mulroy and me. Quite a chunk of change in separate accounts.

Money aside; Mike 2:1 was raring to get some action. I said we were army, navy, marines, air force? We were commandos, zappers, snipers, demolition experts, recon (reconnaissance), seals, paratroopers.

We were younger, older, officers, enlisted, warrant officers and non-commissioned officers (N.C.O.'S) We were a squad which was connected to three other squads that form a company. Et cetera, Et cetera, et cetera.

Upon ourselves, as the most mobile, and strongest unit, capable of accomplishing nearly any mission, with again, no support, we rely.

We would carry Claymores. Ammo for the machine gun: M-60 mortar rounds, M-79 rounds, Fraggs (Fragmentation grenades). Our weapons of choice: .45 Cal., .305 Sniper Rifle. M-16, Auto, Semi-Automatic Assault Rifle. K-Bar—Knife; Bayonet. C-rations. Canteens. Poncho. Sleeping bag. We carried all this gear in rucksack-style backpacks. We carried this gear and we kicked ass. One of us would carry the P.R.C.-25. P.-R.-C.; Radio. Additional Support. Fire Power. Medivac. Re-Supply.

We were going Arctic. We didn't know it in '35; not even '38. We knew we were Arctic Circle bound by 2040. Seems the Polar Caps weren't breaking up. Weren't 'Global-Warm' ('eding). Seems we just made a little Boo-Boo. A little mistake. We entered an Ice Age. Scientists finally figured out the truth: From maybe 1660 A.D. Earth was shaking herself out of an Ice Age. Compared to 2040; 1600 weather was a thaw. Still there was land, oil, food (seals, walruses, polar bears, fish) at the North and South Poles. Enough to fight and die for. Mike; 2:1—Call to Arms...

2:1 for Mike's call digits; may or may not have stood for Second Battalion, First Regiment. It may and it may not have. There are certain things the public has a right to know and there are certain things the general public has no right to know. Right or Wrong. Democracy or Not. Those numbers themselves may not be actual.

SNAKES VI

Frigid perma frost solid-Air. That was what was north. Along with thermal underwear and cars with hardtops and bottoms. We were required to wear cold weather parkas tested to between -40° to -60° below zero. Cold weather parkas and view goggles. Inch-thick plastic lenses to keep the moisture in your eyeballs from solidifying. Wear view goggles, cardhard clothes and cold weather parkas tested to -40° and -60° below zero when you leave the cabins. Thank you very much.

Quonset Huts. Hundreds of them. Hundreds and hundreds of Quonset huts. Cabins. Fifty people per cabin. Work a six-hour shift. Guard duty, mess duty, oilwell duty, oil refinery duty. Rest six hours in the bunk of the twenty-five double bunks assigned you. Shower, shave, eat. Take a G.I. shower. Wet down. Shut water. Soap up. Rinse. Done. Topside.

Below. Beneath the frozen perma-frost tundra, lay the bunker. A ten-square mile of command center corridors: meeting rooms, day rooms, infirmaries, mess-halls, offices, private rooms (quarters), laundry facilities, storage, munitions. Three miles beneath the perma-frost tundra. Reinforced iron girders. Turbine engines supplying enough energy to power a city. Thousands of personnel.

THE SQUAD

Usually a squad is composed of three Fire Teams with four members per team. And our basic Squad Leader, Corpsman/Medic , radio man, and ain't we got fun? So anyway this is my weekly report of status; as far as Mike 2:1 goes: Fat-Boy, Slick, and Jones had served in the army and navy together. Four years navy. Four years Army. Me and Mulroy—four years marines. Murphy and Snakes? Ten years Marines. And it didn't surprise me we were a ragtag team of veterans who ran together; come what may. No, it didn't surprise me much. I've heard of some of the boys doing five years in the four major branches of the military. Twenty and scoot.

Talk about disparity. Slick has a pottery conglomerate. You may have heard of New Wave Ceramics. The "Biggest Dish Wins" group? But the pottery, hollow ceramic snakes in poses of: slumber, hotwing down, a hapless frog caught between the dripping fangs of a snake were all 'the rave.'

Or take Murphy. What began in free Cuba as a Victory Farm has the premium Tobacco Plantation making the Finest Cigar Money Can Buy. Yeah, we walk different paths but our group has the bond that binds—Fraternity. Military fraternity. We're a brotherhood to the last. We're rough and tumble. Tough. Hard. We'll take our four platoons of Chinese regulars. We don't feel like we have anything to lose, by giving our all. We live lives of strict discipline. Rigorous. Demanding. We're "professional bachelors." We've known love. Now we fight. We've been Commandos; Seals; Merchant Marines;

Airborne. We've been these things and we've been more. Much, much more.

Television Repairmen. Electricians. Carpenters. Auto Mechanics—and yes, Virginia, there is a Santa Clause.

Anyway; if Snakes is running thirty miles to set up an ambush; he may or may not be carrying three mortar rounds and the base or tube of the mortar in his pack; two or three bandoleers of machine gun rounds—or 500 rounds each; two, three grenades—hell, we all might ... the machine gun; our own weapons; knives ... Am I missing anything here???

SNAKES VII

Beneath. Below. Heat. Warmth. Exposure to this heat suddenly after enduring the weather above, could act on the central nervous system; like a glass taken from a refrigerator and placed on a stove. Ka-put! You may enter the three-mile-below bunker in three stages:

> First Stage: Four hours with clothes on, one mile down.
> Second Stage: Vigorous workout to bring body temp equal to room temperature; at a low degree.
> Third Stage: Entry to three-mile-deep bunker for 3 months.

"Throw me that Monkey-Wrench; Snakes," I yelled.

He yelled back; "You don't want me to throw you anything that weighs ten pounds..."

"Right." I understood. We were doing pipe fittings under the oil pipe rigging. Hot air pipes. Huge hot air pipes under the oil well rigging. It was warm enough for just our diehards in here. We were in a fifty-square-foot area. Reeves, Slick, Snakes, and me, Eagle. "I'll come get it," I yelled back. By 2040 we'd smartened up. We did not suffer needlessly. We had put fiberboard over Plexiglas to keep out the worst of the cold and wind. And we installed heating and lighting to areas we needed access to. And about the cabins? The Quonset Huts? They were heated with diesel fuel and kerosene. There was never any fire—ever. We could screw fiberboard or plywood to fiberglass easily. Very easily. And that's what we did. The lower portions of the oil well rig were dressed on the structure.

Oil well. Oil Refinery. The Bunker. The Cabins. A heated snowtrac made the patrols and guard duty pathetically easy. Or hunting ... or combat...

There were a whole new set of rules and regulations to Arctic Circle Combat. Declared an 'Enron'; by the United World Chamber meant what was yours and your nation's property you could manage and protect. The Chinese had value here. Russia. America. England. Canada. We thought of ourselves as a unibody. A mainhead with tentacles like a squid or octopus. Clear kill zones. Demilitarized zones. Killing fields. Hands off high voltage security fences topped with razor sharp concertina wire. Three rows thick. With heated, two-man observation posts every fifty feet. For six hours duty. A magnitude of ten square miles of this...

I once asked Snakes why anyone in their right mind would spend ten years in the U.S.M.C.

His answer:

1. I couldn't differentiate between a circumference and a perimeter.
2. I couldn't acquire a taste for good coffee.
3. I challenged myself and ate two dead rats—like women Marines.

Sounds good to me. Where do I sign up?

Arctic Circle Combat. Extreme Circumstance Warfare. Snowshoes. Skis. Added to other survival equipment. But white. Pure white. Pure, pure white. Nothing but snow is seen. Ground snow. Air snow. Mounded snow. White gloves in white mittens. White breathing masks to filter perma-frigid air, and to keep breath from being seen. On a grade or hill stay low. Hide profile. See your enemy. Sense your enemy. Bear down on him. Your sights and white rifle barrel. Take in half of a deep breath; as you take the slack from your trigger in a cool, calm, collected draw (squeeeeeze). Take the shot. Make the kill. Do it once. Do it 10,000 times. Your enemy has 200 million people. And you can jolly well believe he has a good 1 percent of these people (as) comrades-in-arms.

KA-BOOM

Ka-Boom Ka-Boom. Ka-Chinggg!!! I work hard for my two cents. After the nuclear rains we'd gone topsy-turvy in more ways than one. Work eighty-seven hours for two cents? That has the equivalent purchasing power of $1,360.00 before the rains? Pulleeeeees! Gimmee a break. Eight-seven hours to buy a can of water? Who puts the water in the can?? God's sister?

An' ya' tell me folks are droppin' dead in these parts 'cause they're about as smart as turkeys that go out in the rain with their heads thrown back and their mouths open and drown??? Is that what you are telling me??? Ka-Boom. Ka-boom. Ka-Chinggg!!!

And the big all time guarantee they're tryin' ta' make ya' swalla' like so much swill—no more make war!!! Guaranteed!!! At least 'til the next time. So be it. Ya wanna know what I think?

These heads of state or something have been eating too many radiation ice cubes!!! Ka-Boom. Ka-Boom. Ka-Chinggg!!! Ya want my two cents...

I work the slots at quadruple solitaire. Misnomer. You have nuclear holocaust. You can have drop-dead-fred sixtriplet solitaire—as long as boss gives ya' your $.02. I'm not asking you if you like it or not. Am I, Henry??? So take THIS little bit of wisdom to your C.O. You have a dissenting voice among you. Sue me. I'll split my savings right down the middle 30/70.

Ka-Booom. Ka-Boom. Ka-Chinggg...!!!

BEGAT BEGAT HORRENDOUSITY

Trouble begat trouble begat Horrendousity.
    Herman Houast was uneasy. He stood in front of the Victorian Mansion seemingly unconcerned about anything. But Herman Houast shook inside. Shook up. Herman was shook up. His tongue made a dry clicking sound far in the back of his throat. Such was the horrendousity of Herman Houasts' life. Uneasiness, dry throat, seemingly unaware of the cold sweat on his brow...
    The Victorian Mansion stood miles from its nearest neighbor; surrounded on three sides by a fairly dense woods. There is a huge circular driveway in front of Herman's dark house. His "spooky" house. Haunted. The house in which thirty kids were interred within the marble bricks downstairs. Thirty headless kids. Thirty decapitated kids. Herman's bleak ancestry included the Earl of Evil. Superiority of Sinfulness and the Duchess of Depravity. The local villagers are rumored to have heard the shrieks of ruined flesh being shred when the Duchess was 'in her cups.'
    Herman Hoauost struck a match, lit a torch and entered the Gothic living room. Off to his left was the library. The dusty volumes of Faust, Grendel, Whitmourth, and the like excited Herman's senses. The old feelings were beginning to return. Cauldrons of boiling torture oil. The smell of rotting flesh. Huge skin pinchers to rip yielding skin and bone. The head-pounding screams of sound begging for the end of trauma.

Trouble begat trouble begat Horrendousity; but the 'feel' was getting rekindled and beginning after all, hadn't the Duchess been in her cups of late?

SEVEN FEET

My fishing rod is seven-feet long. I'm 5'9" tall, and my fishing rod is seven-feet long. My feet are nine and a half inches long and my fishing rod ... yeah; yeah, yeah, blah, blah, blah.

What I'm giving you are repetitions, measurements, presentations. Let 'em reach out and grab 'ya. I used to hear voices. They told me things. I used to tell my doctors when they hollered orders at me. Like, "Be a fishhook." Or "Put out your cigarette" Or; "Light up a cigarette" in rapid succession. I used to have bad panic attacks and anxiety attacks. I told my doctors that too. I told them all I could do when they struck was breathe in and out...

But anyway, let me get back to my fishing exploits. Of which I knew diddly from day one to the end of last May. Round about November of last year I come to realize a hungry bass might or might not consider a lure with cast out from a seven-foot rod to bass waters fair game. Now what might cast a line into bass territory? A seven foot rod? Cast by a 5'9" guy with 9 1/2" dogs? Yes. Yes indeedy.

VAPORS

The smell of the winery was seeping over me in waves. In a way I thought of it as amusing. A swarm of hornets caught up in the sickly sweet aroma of the wine. This thought was suddenly followed by the much more sobering knowledge that there are thousands in Hell's Kitchen, and the Bowery who might not think bees following a scent as funny.

    I let my mind wander as I walked through these smells. Let's say I wrote four books. Let's say I had a cocktail party after writing each book. I began to think I'd maybe begun to run a little short on story material the more I drank. And then I thought okay. So no one needs your hypothetical bullshit anyway, so quit trying to write "War and Peace II." And I got a little sad because I like to write. I really don't care. (I told myself if people who are drinking read what I write . . .) but I suddenly realized plenty of people would read what I write. Drinking or not. And my happy feelings replaced the negative thoughts quickly. And I thought of something else good and exciting, too. People as books. Yes. Fahrenheit 451 and more. That all people have a story. Or many, many, many of them (as my drill instructor may have said referring to push ups, or some such. So I slept on it. And then I began writing scathing reports about booze:

    Booze-related accidents
    Booze and medicine overdoses
    Raucous Cacophony

And other things along these same lines. Not the least of which my facetious justification to 'pound 'em down.' I'd rather see you have a beer than a shot of whiskey.

A CONSIDERATION

Under collections:

China (Bone)
Sterling Silver
Art
Calculators
Buttons
Broomsticks and doorknobs

John Laidlaw closed his filing cabinet and smiled to himself. He made $50,000 IN THE LAST SIX MOTHS. MNIMAL. He could make $100,000.00 a month. Usually he did. Often. The rich don't speak of money. The wealthy don't speak of riches. John Laidlaw didn't speak of money or riches—more wealthy collections. John Laidlaw bought collections to collect. He bought:

Biscayne bicycles
Scrimshaw Pipes
Marble Chess Sets
Sets of balanced throwing knives
Jewelry
Antiques
Heirlooms

Yeah; John Laidlaw; had sets of balanced throwing

knives; balanced throwing knives with scrimshaw handles. Scrimshaw chess sets. Did I tell you John Laidlaw has Scrimshaw chess sets? That's not all John Laidlaw has blue; and green; and red; Chicago Biscayne bicycles and they're as fast as a car going uphill. Bone China in china cabinets in two or three warehouses. Two or three floors of 5,000 20-story warehouses. Antique furniture. Antique art. Coin collections. Stamp collections. Card collections. Porcelain. Tapestries. Carpets. Antique sterling silver.

John Laidlaw twitched, shook and shuddered. The keys of the warehouses were in the safe in the basement and he had shot some heroin last year? Ten minutes ago? He could no longer trust his memory. What's the combo??? I shot heroin. For what? To be a stoned-assed junkie with a monkey on my back?

JULY

Maybe three months of baseball left. If nobody brakes his neck beforehand in the playoffs. One of the guys got life for playing while on heroin at the end of the season.

Grumpy was watching me. Grandpa Grumpy is not mean. In a grey and brown plaid suit Grandpa Grumpy might look like a college professor. Grandpa Grumpy wore jeans and tee-shirts backwards and picked at his face a lot. Ma and Dad went to Aunt Louise's in Florida. "Gator-ville," Grump said. What Grandpa Grumpy's job was this time was to "bring me to age."

I was weaned from the teat, sent to boys prep school (where we all wore black pants, jackets and shoes) and made the transition from youth to adolescence; from adolescence to young adulthood, all under Grandpa Grumpy's tutelage. Now "I was coming of age." I was going to be sixteen next month and win, lose, or draw, I wasn't going to swap spit with Suzy Rottencrotch. No girls from Cheeles High School. No girls from Walmart. No ticket girl from the Rialto where on a Saturday night you could usually catch a Bogart and Bacall flick. I wasn't a puppy. I felt no love.

A bomb went off under me that July. "I'm no relative of yours, Marty." I stared at the man who was known to me as Grandpa Grumpy. "I'm a hanger-on." I felt a lump in my throat as he continued. "I'll do this 'n' that for people for a bit and move on."

I had tears in my eyes at this point as I said; "Why?"

He paused and looked at the stars and answered, "You know why." And the truth was yes. I did know why. He liked me. He practically raised me like a son. Why? He loved me. This time the tears were in my throat. "Thank you."

DR. ESPOSITO JONES

Dr. Jones looked up from his "patient" who had been screaming violently for the last four hours, and grinned sadistically. He dangled the bloody portion of Alverez Quintezes's fingers over Alverez's head. The fingers had been cut off with Rose Trimmers; and then sliced lengthwise. The fingers were sliced in front of Alverez for the psychological horrifying effect.

But Alverez wouldn't shut up. If Alverez didn't shut it up—and real soon—Dr. Jones was going to shut him up. And THAT would give Alverez something to yell about!

Yes. Yes. Yes. Dr. Jones began his treatment with electrical current. 440 Volts. No treatment was too good for Jones's people. 440 Volts with a bucket of water splashed on a "patient" was next.

Then the toes were cut from the patients. 1,0000 volts of electricity were applied. Dr. Jones had some time ago decided that a writhing patient—from electricity—could make blood spurt from fingers and toes—quite far. Sometimes with grins and giggles, Dr. Jones removed the jawbone and tongue of a patient. Not the teeth though. Not the teeth. They could be used to bite through the still screaming cheeks. More electricity was given to surge through a patient. 3,000 volts. First sans water. Then with a bucket of water. A few years ago Dr. Esposito Jones had discovered a patient under optimum conditions might or might not loosen his bowels and privates, too. Dr. Jones was an angry Doctor.
Mad.

A mad doctor was Dr. Esposito Jones. Blood did gush from patients' noses and other orifices. This triggers the madman in Dr. Esposito. More electric. More fingers. More toes. More screams. Enough was not enough for the good mad doctor. In later times, Dr. Esposito Jones would've been known as Fiend.

At the age of 56, Dr. Esposito Jones stuck a double-barreled shotgun into his mouth and pulled the trigger. Amen and Amen.

BLATTSFORDS PHLATTS

Blattsfords Phlatts, Wyoming wasn't called Blattsfords Phlatts because of the sound you make when you put your lips on your arms and blow. No. It had to do with the Cider Mill on East Main.

A rugged town with hard people, you won't see its like if you travel fifty miles east, west, north, or south. Such is the population of Blattsfords Phlatts. One would bump someone upside his shoulder into another resident and spit on his heel for spite.

Then there was the Mill. The Cider Mill. Many times an employee would go in whistling—if low, and come out half sloshed. Now that ain't right. Half the time the half shift of half the town was at once working, would stumble out of the Mill and into O'Grady's. Now I ain't gonna spell out to ya' O'Grady's is a suds factory.

Yeah.

The barkeep at O'Grady's has a roll of money that'll choke a horse. But can they take it with them when they croak? I don't guess they can. Now you're thinking Blattsfords Phlatts. Blattsfords Phlatts. Where oh where have I heard that name before? Well actually, Blattsfords Phlatts used to be a big ole' doggy town +^$#&. Keep them doggies movin'...

A BAD MISTAKE

John Lawton scratched his head and spat. He was in a parking lot with Louie Vargus. Louie Vargus was patiently trying to explain to John Lawton that he really should try to pay his debts on time.

"If you don't pay your debt next week;" Louie explained reasonably, "I'll send over a guy to break a toe. Every week a toe. When you're out of toes we can start on the first one again. Or we can start on the fingers." Reasonable. Weirdly reasonable.

"Jesus," John Lawton said. "What'd I do?"

"You made a mistake, John." Reasonable. "You made a deal with the devil." This time Louie smiled tenderly.

"You said I could have time," John tried.

"Not my fricken' lifetime. You give me $5,000.00 next week or one of your toes will pay."

Awww geeee, John Lawton thought miserably. *I'm going to be sick.*

"You don't want to disappoint me, John. I'm counting on you."

John Lawton robbed a bank. He was shot trying to get away. He felt like he had "made a deal with the devil!!!"

LILLITH GRENDEL

Work the words, Lillith. Bring forth Klath. Klath the destroyer. Klath who had wiped out humanity with his broadsword. Work the words, Lillith. Invoke the curse that will endure past time.

Invoke the curse that within its mighty fire will forge a new Klath, who, it was foretold will destroy the mighty kingdoms of life.

Destroy, Lillith. With Klath at your side destroy the infidels who would cling to meager lives as though, enjoying.

Destroy the foundations of existence to fulfill carnal need; between yourself and your moxie Klath.

Breeding and bred. Kin and friend, wiped out. The adventurous and the timid alike; woebegone... Woefully, woebegone...

Now eternity time is like here. Time eternal. Dawn of man. Apocalypse. Alpha-Omega. Everything and anything in between. No horror—too slight—too great. From the great torture racks of Dark Ages Europe to the prisoner war camps of Asia, and modern Europe, Lillith and Klath, frolicked, unconcerned, uncaring. Different names, age to age, but the message is the same: mayhem, gore, gristle.

Work the wars, Lillith. Work the four horsemen of the Apocalypse with Klath.

Famine pestilence, fire, war! All work no play makes Jack a dull boy! Work the wars, Lillith, Klath. Have a little fun...

BILLIE BILLIE

Billie held Barney and Alice on her knees. They were cooing to each other. Barney acted for a moment like he wanted nothing more in the world than acquiring the pacifier sticking out of Alice's mouth.

Alice kicked stubby legs at him to ward her brother off.

Billie didn't pay any attention to the kids. She was used to the siblings struggle. Billie watched the people in the mall. She listened and watched. The noises and sights swam in and out of her eyes and ears. The sights and sounds swam in and out of Barney's and Alice's eyes and ears as they struggled too. They seemed oblivious to their surroundings.

Billie was getting a new Dodge pickup; and coasting on a carpet of excitement. She'd met John six months ago and John had taken control of the roller coaster of domestic violence by Billie's husband, Eric. They were separated anyway, but the calls came: accusations, drunken visits. John strongly suggested Eric blow the coop. The divorce was settled last week. John set about alleviating all and any problems in Billie's life. A tear slid from her eye.

THANKLESS

Harry Harroldson began to sweat. Harry didn't begin to sweat because he was pumping iron. No. Harry was scared just about out of his skin. He was scared of the way he might react if that hairy, Chewbacca-like character with its eight-inch needle teeth came around again. Sure, he'd give a banshee bloodcurdling cry. But that would be more for the element of surprise—to catch Chewy off guard, more than anything else.

You think I'm kidding you? You don't know Harry like I know Harry. He was arrested for reckless endangerment once, for trying to jump off the Golden Gate Bridge. Poor Harry. He would have been wearing his knees for elbows. But that's Harry. He planned to "ace" Chewbacca by whacking it across the bridge of its nose and simultaneously driving his other palm upward into the broken gristle, cartilage and bone. Pushing all of the above into its brain.

He didn't reckon on the stench factor. This close up it stank. It was hairy and sweaty, it smelled wild. Harry went to chop the bridge of its nose, lost the advantage from the stench, pushed his hand in the ape's mouth, lost the hand, and consequently—died.

STAR STRUCK

It was Tuesday. He was supposed to be at the hospital Tuesday at 10:00 A.M. Be at Dr. Wendall's office at 10 o'clock Tuesday morning. He was told the incredible pressure in his lung was (as the x-ray showed), a key. A friggin' key! Yes, he slept with his mouth open. Yes, he had a loose parrot that was mad at him. A lot of what happened to Ray Platt that day was my fault. I blabbed about the key. You might say, this was something like someone letting the cat out of the bag!

I'm in Hardwick Penitentiary and I'll never be released. I told Joe Monroe, Ray Platt's mortal enemy, that Ray had swallowed the safety deposit box key—thanks to Kenshaw the cranky parrot, talks in his sleep. He durn near choked on it. The safety deposit box contained 1,000 shares of blue chip stock from a Forbes 500 Company worth tens of millions of dollars.

Seems Ray Platt never made it to Dr. Wendall's office. Seems Ray Platt was found in a filthy alley with his lungs cut open, and a bloody linoleum cutter nearby. No key. No safety deposit box key. Imagine that.

Seems the police knocked on my door and said, "Mr. John Platt? Ray Platt's brother? We'd like to ask you some questions."

BA-WA-NA JR.

The natives called me Ba-Wa-Na Jr. I don't know why. I didn't do anything to anyone. Maybe I should have done something for someone—and didn't. I'm kept in a cage. In a cage I'm kept. Now I'm fed. I was made to understand I'm to suck a granule of rice for nourishment. Protein. I'm given three pieces of rice a week.

"I'm given pen and paper; and the natives think it's quite funny to see me write words.

For some amazing reason these people dress in monkey skins and dance around my cage. They throw sticks at me. They throw rocks at me. At times these people force me to run. Run. Run. Run. Run. Until I'm in a daze. A trance.

On these forced runs one could very well imagine endorphins going haywire. Runners high. Not so. Not even close.

The mean temperature in the day climbs to 120–124. In the night the coolest air is 100 degrees.

For some other amazing reason; these people put on dog fur and dance around my cage; and bark and growl. They claw me and bite me. They throw at me; what only can be construed as entrails … guts … blood …

I don't know how much more of this I can take. I've been here—what? Two decades? Twenty years? A generation? I bet I've been here a generation. "Help me! Drop the bomb. Drop the bomb. From the day of the mighty swashbuckler—all for one, one for all … Please I've lost my humanity. I'm less than a gutter rat. I'm toothless. I'm encrusted in filth. Oh, no! Everyone is running around looking for a weapon—we're being invaded; Crymmminnnyy.

THE BEAR WITH THREE PAWS

We were getting no closer to a solution to what had happened to Clyde Weisblott's bear paw. Actually we knew what happened to one claw. It was stuck up in a tree by Clyde's house, his 'Neck 'O the Woods.' The Department of Forestry knew not how it had gotten ten feet up a tree. A bear paw and part of the attendant limb and nothing more.
A zoologist from the county seat in Auburn, Georgia didn't shed any light on it. I felt bad about that but Sandy Cruthers said; "I'll buy 'ya a drink, Geoffrey."
 "I'm Geoffrey Collins and the night Clyde crashed his truck looking up at trees with bear paws, on a mild June night, I had come along and witnessed it with Clyde.
 "So whaddya' get when ya' rub two Hillbilly's together?" Sandy Cruthers didn't have to make heh heh to make me like the way she fit her tight blue jeans. It had been a fine day. "What?" I asked through a mild haze of cold Guiness. "Smoke?" Her laughter drowned out mine. It was funny. Two days later we knew what happened to that poor bear.
 "Every, maybe, five years we hear it." I was looking at the local meteorologist with my jaw dropped. I knew I must look ridiculous but c'mon... " Lightning hit the leg of that bear and made a paraplegic of it?" "Yeah." "I went to where you said it happened and there are burn marks in the bark. The fur on the bear leg is burnt."
 So the great riddle of Clyde's bear was solved. "It'll die; Geof. It'll die and next year there will be thirty full-grown

whole bears out there, where the deer and the antelope play..."

I wanted to see Sandy Cruthers before she went back to Auburn. I went where we had had ice cold Guiness and asked the waitress where she was. "Haven't seen 'er, darlin'."

A couple of the locals were hitting some balls around on the pool table. "Hey, look'y here. It's the bear boy. Why don't you get bare, boy?" Sally walked in. I hit the loudmouth in the face with the cue and ordered a cold Guiness for me and Sally.

THE CAR

I was dreaming that I was at some railroad tracks. I was real tired because I had come a long way. I looked left. No train. I looked right; and a humungous cacophony of air horns blew through my head. It was my alarm clock. I had a drive of 150 miles ahead of me.

I'm a businessman and me and four other men were going up to the cabin I own in the Adirondack Mountains, about as I said, 150 miles north of Albany. Business had been fierce for three years. Reality. People all over the world were coming to "The Land of Opportunity" to buy property and settle down.

John tells him he's full of shit. I looked at the left rear seat at Tom Adele and smiled. He had just been measuring how far he wanted to believe there were three-legged bear in the woods up north. Larry Smathers, in the "shotgun seat" had just so advised Tom Adele.

"Actually Larry's got a point," I told them. We were probably thirty miles out of Albany and that dream was still nagging at me. My station wagon was humming along. "There's been documentation," I continued. "People are moving in on the bears' land, crowding them out. Getting them worked up. They're doing what they wouldn't otherwise," I continued. "Sleep on railroad tracks. Climb a tree in a lightning storm. Go into peoples' camps. They go mad." I said this. I said this and there were other things I didn't say. A mother bear will protect her cubs to the death. I'd read a bear will circle around and attack a hunter from the rear. Wonder if a starving bear would eat part of another bear?

UH OH

Yeah, Sally from the Department of Environment Sciences had told me sometimes because of people encroaching bear land, bear would get skittish—maybe climb a tree in a lightning storm. From having been nervous and skittish for much too long, from the encroachment of bear land by human beings, be very, very tired and maybe fall sound asleep on train tracks?

Well, anyway, where was I? Oh. Polecat. Ya' asked me where I thought the word polecat might'a come from. Well let me ask you something. What good is a three-legged bear that maybe lost a paw in a lightning storm in a tree? Eat? Yeah. Sleep? Yeah. Roam? Uh huh. But what in the tarnation might a big, mean, angry, three-legged bear Go after? A fast, scared of it, female bear? Or a cougar maybe that just got through eating? Farmer Brown's prized pig? The big, fat pig that would just make you love to curl in a ball and, s-l-e-e-p? One that maybe a bear in all its bareness might pounce on???

ELIXER

I'd drunk everything within reach. It started out as a wild ride down winding backroads in the hills of Tennessee. Maggee, Tennessee. As opposed to Maggee, Mississippi. Well anyway, and to get back to my story of having drunk everything within reach, I was pretty well lit.

There was Barbara Sue Anderson with me. Sally Kenshaw. And Debby Collins. Yeah. Three girls and me.

And ya' wanna know the funny part? The girls didn't drink! Fudge-a-migudgeit! But the girls smoked. They smoked!!! Did they ever ... I guess some of the nonsense joking around started when I said in my alto sax voice, how we were going up into the sticks where they drink really clear water that does strange things to you, from earthen jugs with three X-es on them. Boy did those gals think that was a hoot!

And I could have safely turned the car around and got to town. Even two or three hours later. But the girls thought I was a hoot. Then things got fuzzy for a while and suddenly, all the girls had on were T-Shirts. Wet T-Shirts. And from somewhere there had sprung a leak of ten or fifteen guys. But hey, the girls were giving it up for the guys. Laughing. Laughing. Laughing. And the guys? Why they were all drinking out of jugs marked XXX and pickin' an' a' grinnin' as ole' Grampa woulda' said.

Now don't get me wrong. I ain't queer or what they call gay, but I heard about Consolidated industries in Maggee,

Mississippi and Maggee, Tennessee and it ain't no coincidence that industry starts with con...

And besides, I felt some responsibility for these young vixens. Oh, there I go again; showing my natural predaliction for the fine-eerrrhhh-uuuuhhhnhh nice young ladies. Besides I had to see that these young men went no further than makin' the girls laugh it up a bit. I guess I passed out. When I felt better and I had my wits about me, I gathered the girls up and drove them back to town. It's funny though. They had nothing to drink and yet they smelled like a distillery. What's up with that???

THE TELEVISION

Three people talking on the TV. They were all talking at once. "Deemer, are you listening to me?" A ruddy director looked like he wanted nothing more than to punch out Deemer's lights. He had Deemer's lapels in his pudgy hands and was shaking him; violently while spraying a thick stream of spittle.

"Let 'im go, Max." Now it was the guy in the green suit puling on Max's forearms. "You're going to shake his head right off."

"Yeah, right," Max answered John, the assistant stagehand who was wearing the too tight-green suit. Probably a fag.

Just to show he had no hard feelings; Max gave Deemer a pat on the back. "No hard feelings, eh Deemer?" Just then an amazing thing happened. A cherry pit popped out of Deemer's open mouth.

The script had called for a toga party with scantily dressed Egyptian women lounging around Roman hot baths hand feeding the victorious gladiators grapes, figs, cherries...

"Look, Deemer, you tell me you want me to can the kid for shoving cherries down your throat or you're gonna walk out on me?"

"Well the girls have a three-movie contract. What am I supposed to do? Walk out on that? And besides, Deemer's contract we'd have to have a bunch of extras close-ups."

"I didn't mean to get rough. I sort of knew something

was in the wind when you went blue in the face. "We'll work it out. We'll work it out...."

I chronicled this, Deemer walked. Left the studio. Left Rome? Who knows?

"Who cares?" Max said. "The next time; we use olives..."

THE TREE II

The bus came by every day at half past the hour. The tree wasn't at odds with itself about a bus or time as it was as tall as the five-story hospital before which it stood. The tree felt it was above such PICAYUNE business. It knew. It knew. The tree knew it lived in a small town and it had seen its fair share of people come and go, literally perhaps.

The tree was on a mission. It was the tree's mission to be an epic. A book. A novel of a love and beauty so great that it hadn't been spoken of since the days of Shakespeare. The Lord of God himself spoken of and speaking through the Bible itself. The tree was choosing himself to be as the fine pulp which he would be formed as fine paper. The story of the ages would be written upon it for all humanity to read.

The tree studied its situation. Obviously, it must be cut down. It was the cutting that preoccupied the tree. A chainsaw wasn't going to be that harsh. It would think mower; at the crucial period. Or snowblower, as the teeth bit hungrily, it would remember, children yelling as they played ball. Yes, this took planning, this took—time. The tree would remember the cry of the siren of the ambulance and the second; third; twentieth centuries, chances for folks to relax. Relax and come to their senses in a well-written novel.

Oh, no! I feel people in me. On me. Oh, God, no. They made a house out of me. Are you crazy? Wipe your feet! No smoking! No smoking! Stop yelling!

THE COUCH

Mary Lou had been nagging me about lounging around. "Get busy. Do something. You're always lounging around on that damn couch." She was right of course. I go to school at night and I go to a Vet Center during the day and I'm trying to write the next; 'Great American Novel.' But Mary Lou's right. Every chance I get I stretch out on the couch.

There was a time I didn't lie around. I can't remember when. It's the medicine. I take medicine to help me forget. I forget so much. I forget to take my medicine sometimes. I suppose you can forget just about anything. Anyway the couch makes me happy. Surprised? It's not just that I can take a nap on it; it makes me feel whole. I lost an arm in Vietnam. Did I forget to tell you? I'm over the heartbreak. Flashbacks. I don't flinch when a car backfires. The couch helps me forget.

Medicine and the couch. And people. Certain people will take a chunk of memory out of me. Like a therapist. I've got about four counselors and they're helping me rebuild a life gone sour.

They're tricky though. Like this Captain. I was explaining how a captain had called evacuation on a mission. I was just begging to sink my teeth into, then the counselor disappears and the couch appears.

My God! Mary Lou looks like she's had her thorax torn out by a rabid werewolf. I'm going to have to take a little nap.

BEHAVIOR

"Behave, honey." I kissed my daughter on her forehead and smiled down at her. She smiled back at me and said, "Behave, Bob." This time I laughed. Sally knew my heart. Sally knew my heart revolved around her. I kissed my wife Mary at the door and said, "Our little girl is growing up."

"Bob, she's four years old. She isn't growing up." Mary is a pragmatist and practical.

"True," I said, "I'm the one getting old." I went to work. I work at the gun factory downtown.

Five or six guys were in the break room when lunch began. Half hour. Sure Shot Guns didn't break long. "Took that bastard in mid-hop." Harry Coolander was re-hashing for the fourth time since the weekend how he had bagged a jack-a-lope with a .30 x.30. A jack rabbit. Jack-a-lope. A booking ass jack rabbit. Loping, loping, like trying to escape the claw of the falcon, the tooth of the coyote.

Puffing out his chest, Harry Coolander said, "I'll stuff it and stick it in the mouth of that prairie dog I bagged last year."

"Yeah, Harry. And about 'bagged'—you're usually half in the bag. Got lucky with a shot," I continued. "And now you seem to think we give a shit about you letting the gas out of the bag or not." I was pumped. Harry's big but he's stupid. God's work—not mine.

"Hey, take your best shot." He stuck out his chin.

"I just did, Harry."
He actually flushed and flinched.
Again God's work.

COMFORTABLE

The trouble with feeling comfortable is sometime, somewhere the comfort comes to an end.
    I'm a Madison Avenue Executive and what I'm talking about here is basically, my plush life came crashing down around my ears, and there was not a thing I could do about it. I was a Mad. Ave. Exec. in the manner of a Corporate Stock Broker and my magic carpet was pulled out from beneath me. Samuel Gristwald, III of Gristwald, Gristwald, and Smith called me to his office and in a no-nonsense tone told me I was being let loose ... Gold Cigar, Brass Watch, that sort of thing. Okay. I was a Mad. Ave. Exec. this morning and the door slammed me in my face as the day wore on.
    I have nominal wealth so I'll survive however long it takes me to become re-employed. I've secretly been taking classes to become a physician. A doctor. My first patients are to be, coincidentally, Gristwald, Gristwald, and Smith. Okay.
    I was a Mad. Ave. Exec. last week and now I've got three metal gurneys with three sets of straps on each and blood troughs running around the sides. And yeah. I got Chloroform and yeah, I'm strong enough to carry an unconscious man from say, an office to a car. And yes, coincidentally enough, it seems these three persons in question want my incredible genius back in their offices. Imagine that!
    I was a Madison Avenue Executive ten years ago, and before that I was a model prisoner in Yates State Penitentiary. I was so good ... the trustees put me in sick bay as an attendant

and I partially learned a trade. Well, I'm back in the pen and I have been ten year learning this trade—writing. Well with one thing becoming another, seems coincidentally enough here were three comfortable Mad. Ave. Execs. found that had endured a lot of discomfort before being discovered in those sewers. And now ... I'm quite comfortable...

CONSISTENCY

The grey matter between one's ears has the consistency of pudding at room temperature. Alright, you're rather picayune and you'd rather not consider pudding at room temperature, but rather, chilled. At maybe at 30° Fahrenheit? Fine. Fine. Fine. Fine. But the main subject matter of what we're discussing here is the most important organ in the human body. The brain. Cranium. Medulla Oblongata. Skull-housing. Headshot. Gourde. Weather chilled or room temperature, vital.

No two snowflakes alike, no two brains alike? Siamese twins are head to head. Two who share same brain? Aha. I think we may have something here. A shared brain? Twice as warm? Two bodies supplying blood to the brain? How warm? What's the consistency here? Hmm?

Well, seems there's a bit more of a discrepancy in consistency here than meets the eye. Take blood. As in blood transfusion. You want the right consistency. Yes, you sure do. What if the blood in you is lighter than the blood in the transfusion? Guess your blood is absorbed into the heavier blood. I don't know. I'm not a doctor. Then this consistency of blood circulates through your body into your brain; only this combination of your blood and the transfusion blood is heavier, and combined, warmer? Making one feel—what? A leaden down feeling?

Yes, maybe you look a little lopsided. And the doctor sees you looking a little lopsided-looking and gives you a pill.

And now things really begin to heat up. So you what? Cry a little more frequently? I don't know. I'm not a doctor.

So. Your brain is overheating. You're tilted. Your brain is mush. And you cry a lot. Prognosis? An adjustment period of four or five years. Hospitalization. An answer. Finally an answer. Diagnosis: Shock Treatment. Although I'm leery of using treatment as in nice, with shock, I'm sure it's wondrous. I've enemies of enemies given treatment. Curl your short hairs. I don't know. I'm not a doctor.

DIARY

Diary didn't start out "Dear Diary." Diary started out "I need help... and I need help in a big way."

In Vietnam in code, if you needed help you said, spell me. Thirty years ago if you needed help you said, spell me. But like I said that was thirty years ago and this is thirty years later.

And I am in a fix. I am in a fix because the young of this day and age (when you say; 'spell me') take it to mean cast a spell on me. Not I need help for a reason very much like being under a spell.

I've suffered with schizophrenia; 'lo these thirty years. Panic attacks. Anxiety attacks. And sometimes all three all at once. No, I need no 'spell' cast on me. Schizophrenia, at least the schizophrenia I'm cursed with, contains its own dose of nasties. Some of the 'nasties' that put me a cut above, Spells? Stasis. Can't move. About the only capability, breathe in and out—slowly. Stiffness. Best case scenario in this case: roll in protective ball to protect head, heart, main arteries, in legs. 'Voices.' Sounds sounding like orders being shouted in my mind. Pain. Pain, unmentionable. Excruciating. The only relief for this unremitting sensation is to shriek as though a rupture in a large beast.

Diary I need help. I invoke anyone who sees diary, to help my misery. No more anxiety. No more panic. No stasis—not for a while. And yet... a pall of doom overshadowing my day/night. No schizophrenia for sometime now, but paranoia! Alas! Paranoia as bright as a noonday in June. HELP! Is the bayonet even now approaching the soft connection in back of me between head and neck.

Bullet traveling 3,273 ft. per second? Had I gone too far with the nifty razor some time back? Did I invoke Geronimo's curse? Did I break rank and order on the front line of some God-Forsaken military campaign or other? Why me? Oh woe is me...

I'd known I was cheating. I'd known since the early times. People call them Prehistoric times.

I had muddled through the Dark Ages; causing mischief and mayhem alike as much for something to do as not. I have never known, even in my wildest calculations, whether or not I was Cro-Magnum Man or Neanderthal. I've had beards through the ages and I've been shorn of facial hair. This is unimportant. What is important is you have to help me regulate my far drifted farsightedness as I am unable to discover what lies ahead as I was for the eons since the dawn of man...

Help me here ... can this be the end? I smell ozone mixed with isotopes ... oh God ... Nuclear Waste.

MONSTER MAKER

Monster Maker isn't a machine. Monster Maker isn't something you can put gas in and wind up and let go. No; Monster Maker is a mad man. Monster Maker is a mad doctor, if you will. He wasn't always a bad sort. A bad guy. Phillip Mongolis was a physical therapist over the edge. Around the bend.

Phillip Mongolis has terrible secrets. Haven't we all got terrible secrets? The Monster Maker Phillip Mongolis strung people by their feet from lampposts. The Monster Maker worked the masses to stone the strung-up people. Pelted with rock and stick, Monster Maker made the strung up people curse upside down to a nether-God. Some bad secrets? You would ask of some of the bad secrets of Monster Maker? Breaking the legs of cats and dogs is bad. Punching and kicking dogs and cats in the head is bad. Throwing women and the infirm from windows is not good—no, not good at all.

Phillip Mongolis has two pet alligators. If not friends, exactly, the gators know him. Phillp Mongolis rules with an iron fist. He feeds the gators horsemeat. The townspeople know that and give him a wide berth. The townspeople run low on horsemeat from time to time. In such an event, the slow villagers donate a nice, juicy leg. A muscular townie might have to part with a leg and arm. The villagers have thusly learned to keep a ready supply of horsemeat.

Yeah, Monster Maker has a fully equipped bunker seven stories below the barn. Few have survived the bunker. Those who do are calculated to spread fear, panic, and riot throughout the land. Beware: Philip Mongolis aka Monster Maker, knows his alligators in case you were wondering.

SUPER

The tenement stood apart from neighboring dwellings by empty lots stretching four blocks in all directions. The tenement was four floors high, with balconies on all the apartments. There was little heat in the winter, and barely a draft of fresh air drifted in through the dirty windows in the summer. The plumbing was stubborn, and the dipsy-dumpsters in back were only irregularly emptied.

Sam Morningstar had hooded eyes, a big hooked nose, puffy thick lips, and small ears. Some say Sam Morningstar is ninety-seven years old. Thick, glossy, black hair tumbled haphazardly down to his big shoulders. Sam Morningstar is the superintendent of 28 Hourglass Road.

The tenement at 28 Hourglass Road also boasts a rickety-looking, rusty, fire escape. There is a dubious looking sprinkler system running up one hallway and down another.

At the moment Archie Benson is complaining to Sam Morningstar. "The pipes got air in 'em, Morninstar."

Samuel Morningstar snickered inwardly and said; "Sioux me."

"Shit." Archie swore under his breath. He knew Samuel Morningstar had used the tribal word for his answer to Archie's problem.

"I'll sue 'ya. I'll burn this dump to ashes."

"Sure;" Samuel Morningstar said; "You just do that." And turned and walked away.

Samuel Morningstar saw "things" in smoke. In his room

by the boiler in the basement, he now saw Archie Benson looking for all the world like the last thing on his mind was burning down 28 Hourglass Road. Instead; Samuel Morningstar saw that weasel Benson impaled by a stake. Hands tied behind his back, naked and burning, trying to scream himself unconscious.

For the first time in quite a while; Samuel Morningstar smiled a shit-eating grin.

THE BOOK

John Johnson has the plan of plans concerning book writing. For one thing he has for the life of him; been sectioning books to read at his station. He works the Ion Tube Displacement Department in Nuclear Power, Heminsford, North Dakota. His reading downtime would be seriously interrupted for quite some time in the event of a meltdown, so he beat the system about that. Bring in what? Sixty pages of a book to breeze through?

Yes, bring in sixty pages of a book to breeze through; in the event a meltdown goes down, somewhat like the fifty-seven times it has happened; in the last six months since John Johnson took up his position at the Ion Tube Displacement Department in Nuclear Power, Heminsford, N.D.

TRAUMA

Billy is ten years old. Billy is ten years old and he is going through a traumatic time of life: childhood to young adolescence. For one thing, although in young Billy's eyes it might be wiser to say, maybe from childhood to boyhood.

Billy has one big variety of secrets he wouldn't divulge if his life depended on it. There was old Mr. Richter. Mr. Rigor-Mortis, Johnny said. Every once in a while Billy struck Mr. Richter in the left knee with a hammer. Hard. Mr. Richter didn't scream—Billy cut out his tongue quite some time ago.

He screamed at first when Billy crushed his ankle with a hammer over and over for not sticking out his tongue for Billy to cut off. And there was Mr. Saxon. Mr. Saxon had no eyes. Billy wanted to see what it felt like to push his fingers in somebody's eye sockets until the eyeballs left the face. Ugh. Sometimes when the mood moved Billy, he shoved a burning candle in the holes in Mr. Saxon's face. Yeah. Billy's quite a character.

He'd cut out Mr. Saxon's tongue also. And there was Agatha. Agatha had no fingers thanks to a pair of Rose trimmers. Didn't she squawk when Billy went for her.

You see, I'm Dr. Harry Furguson; court-appointed psychiatrist for Billy. Billy Meaney. He will be the youngest convict to receive the electric chair. He will fry at 4 A.M. Billy has no remorse. He thinks 'boyish good looks' are cri-minal; and doesn't see why all these older-type people want to fondle him.

TOUR BUS

Groupie Bus: more than that. I own the Tour Bus; and it's the equivalent of a Greyhound Bus and more. On the backs of the seats left, and the backs of the seats right, there are little fold-down tables like on airplanes. And; there's a refrigerator and a microwave oven (careful with the microwave—a fire extinguisher is provided free, non-gratis) and of course the overhead compartments.

The Bus cost $265,000.00. I've quadrupled that every year for the six years I've owned it.

Riding the Tour Bus from coast to coast? $1,000.00. Prerequisite to reserving a seat? Having published a book. Being an author. Being a writer....

The cost of the trip pays for the fuel, meals, repairs. You buy your own souvenirs. And you pay the driver. The driver gets $100.000 from each of the twenty writers or passengers on the Tour Bus. I'm the driver.

Roy "Shank" Williams tells me the stories of what went on in let's say seat four at 2 A.M.

Mandy Armstrong had seen Roy Williams' greedy eyes, trying to look through the too tight yellow velour sweater setting on her too small frame. So yeah. Like so many other sweet nubile before her, Mandy Armstrong lifted the sweater and gave Roy something to really lick, errh ... auuhhh ... look at; something to really write home about.

Meanwhile; Roy "Shank" Williams thought these tarts thought they were giving a late night peep show when in all reality they were auditioning a future script written on the Tour Bus.

And I didn't care. As long as Roy didn't leave out any of the juicy parts when repeating the events on the Tour Bus to me.

ROILED

The water was going to be roiling and it was beginning to come to a boil now. In the water, in the five-gallon pot, were two lobsters. Chet Alter and Bill Armstrong were watching. They were watching the pot closely.

"Why do you do it this way, Chet?" Bill Armstrong was well aware the two lobsters suffered. Chet had not brought the water to a frothing boil and submerged the lobsters.

"Who cares; Bill?" Chet pushed one of the lobsters back down in the pot. "They're nothing but a couple of D.O.A. shellfish ten minutes from now. Quit sniffling."

"Oh shit. I don't care if you pull the arms and legs off the bastards, and roast 'em right over the fire." Bill started to get mean. It's tough to be hard on a bud when you're looking forward to some succulent seafood.

Bill said, "I'll be back."

"Where are 'ya going?"

"Get some crabs;" Bill countered. He needed a minute or two. Yes. They'd walked down to the beach. And yes; there'd been a bright moon. And yes; again, Chet had only two toes and part of his right foot.

Bill wasn't the smartest kid in class; but he knew better than to ask Chet if he had stepped in a bear trap. Shit. And what was going on with the bright-red shellfish aka Lobsters Chet forced down, down, down?

A lobster claw might or might not, out of a whole foot make a half foot with two toes.

Yes. A bright-red shellfish, aka lobster, might or might not, out of a whole foot, make a half foot, with two toes. Yes indeedy. A little action like that might make buddy-boy Chet just a wee bit cantankerous. Yes, oh yes, indeedy.

BO JANGLES

There was going to be trouble again—sure as—**—Fire. There was trouble that time those boys tried ta' get that soldier to drink with 'em. The one all busted up. Only one leg. Lost the other one in the war. Other what? Leg, dummy. Pay attention. What war? What war? Desert Storm, dummy. And it don't make any difference anyway. You should never make someone do something they don't wanna' do. Besides; it wasn't until he blew up the gas station that we knew he didn't want trouble. He'd had his fill of trouble in the army. We jumped him like jackals. Vultures. And now there was going to be trouble all over again.

Some people say people got a "Nervous" condition. Or Battle Fatigue. Or Shell Shock. I think a lot of these guys and gals have head trauma. I think if you could just put 'em at ease with kindred spirits—why you've just invented the better mousetrap that supposedly would the world beat a path to your door!

"What? You think I'm cuckoo? Fine. Do it your way. When ya' start ta' run a little low on gas stations, tell 'em Willie said, "Don't do this, and stop doing that, and let im' alone ... Do you know what a garrison belt is? In the natural order of life a belt holds up your pants. Or keeps your belly flat? Holds your guts in.

Well take a double wide, quadruple wide Garrison Belt to hold in your blood as a field dressing. A tourniquet? Yeah. These half-mad veterans ain't worried that you'll get 'em blitzed. They're hoping when they hit the fan they have some restraint. Now 'ya say I'm talking out of my butt hole. Okay. Ya' hear the one about pushing someone over the line? Now you will really think of me as goofy. I hope if I push someone over the line it isn't what this guy or gal thinks of as a 'front line.'

What's going to trigger the next mayhem? Monkey see/monkey do? A vet retired/combat—who cares? Sees a pattern. Joe Blough goes up for a beer. The vet watches the eyes of the other patrons. He sees three other guys watching the guy at counter. What's this? The guy at the counter has four bottles of brew. A coincidence? I suspect if in any way the dude at the counter had come under "challenge" … there'd been mayhem. And not the reasonable restrained mayhem of a vet.

NEVER MORE

There's no song and dance connected with this story; unlike some of the ones I've written lately.

It began on a dire meeting between me and them Larvae as big as this room. The smell! The stench could be cut with a knife. You'd be mad to want to cut this stench. I was nearly mad after encountering these—things. They were under the stadium. I had needed a place to spend a few hours, so I went down a wet/nasty corridor dark as night, trying not to choke. The first sensation beyond the freezing, stinking air, I became aware of was a mewling. The kind of sound one hears if an eighteen-wheeler smashed into a cow, leaving it in the road mangled, yet still alive. I can't ... I can't go on ... God forgive me. Didn't know what I was seeing. I'd gone into the mouth of that cursed tunnel until I saw things. Vague at first. Outlines. There was a glimmer of shadow from what I took to be fluorescence on the wet tunnel walls. I was two miles into the stadium under/belly. I spoke of an eighteen-wheeler hitting a cow. These cursed slugs were themselves as big as lorries. They were doing things I'll go stark raving mad about if I say it here. I'm going to say it. God damn me—I'm going to say it—they were mingling. UUUHHHhhhh. OOOOhhhhhh.

Frantic to be out and away from these monstrosities I called on my last resources of rationality. I must lure these hideous creatures to the light of day. Pelting them with stones and rocks 'til my fingers bled fiercely; yelling and hollering until hoarse they came at me. God save me! They came at me for I had breached their chamber. Their sanctuary. Screeching and mewling they stretched and retracted and retracted and stretched. I'll go mad if I picture what I'd been about. What action could I take if the sun, the glorious sun, was covered in an early day haze or worse. It wasn't daytime?

I now faced another situation. The tunnel divided ahead. I thought, that can't be right. There was no division coming in. Then there was the only one tunnel—the one with gigantic snail-slugs looking to slurp me in.

The sun—The glorious sun was out. Even the heat of day was shriveling these mutants up. I actually wept. I'm home now and I don't go trotting down long, dark, wet, tunnels.

NO NO NO

Things were beginning to happen again; and I had to lay down the law. Things were not going to happen again. No. No. No. Call it Ecto-Plasma—like in Ghost Busters. Call it Bubble Jel. Call it Three Sheets to the Wind. I don't much care what you call going on about me if you'll help me rid myself of this jam I'm in. No ... No ... No ... the big guy on the totem pole had been pole-axed and didn't much care for THAT scenario.

Mrs. Renquist wasn't a big guy whatsoever. A doctor? Smart? Attractive? You'll give her all that, but she's no guy. No ... No ... No ... Above I began talking about a jam I'm in as though jam was a verb. I mean jam as a noun. My predicament could conceivably conclude with the help of Dr. Renquist. Or not. My predicament could continue ad infinitem ... for eternity. I've had an Emollient implanted within me. I grow weaker by the moment. I don't necessarily blame Dr. Renquist for my troubles; ideally she was unaware this substance was introduced into my circulatory system. I'm praying no other doctor is aware my immunology; is low statis. I pray no other doctor is aware of this as my resistance is real low. The poke of a needle would be the equivalent to a normal man of a point blank gunshot. ... No ... No ... No.

Feelings began to ebb when first these ongoing systems seemed to remove my ability to restore something even as small as weariness by the taking of a small nap. It's like my body or mind were saying, "Nothing doing buddy." It was a case of gritting out the minutes, hours, days beyond that; and as far back as I can look into this continual nightmare. I'll be okay though. If Janice Renquist can discover an anecdote I'll be just fine. Dr. Renquist; with her fine, dark ... No ... No ... No...

Isn't this how a lot of this corrosion, my secret love for Janice unnhhh; uuurrrhhh; ahhhh ... got started to begin with? Jesus, you knew where you were, but what were you thinking...?

So get to, buddy!! Snap to, Luey. And ain't it also true you lay it all on the line by making your mark at the 'X'; for the will, leaving Janice sole heir. Good Christ man. Did your personal trainer just come in and say, "A call from a 'Janice Renquist' calling long distance from Hawaii???"

LUMBER

I was a ball boy for a Little League team. We all were at one time or another. We're the ones who stand along the first base line or the third base line and grab foul balls and roll them to the homeplate umpire. But as we get a little older, say in our teens, we might get put on a double or triple 'A' team to bring a batter one of his bats if he breaks one, or it goes flying off into the stands. Teach ya' ta duck next time, Mabel.

Anyway, a bat was designated "lumber." If you're "packing lumber" you're getting a lot of hits or runs.

Lumber yard? Baseball stadium. Baseball stadium is a real, real good thing. Baseball is America's Great American Pastime.

Problem is, Baseball stadiums remind me of the Roman Coliseums. Don't ask me why. Spectator sport. Things get lost in the translation. Batter Up.

SOMETIMES

Sometimes I ask myself if I feel like a lucky punk. Mostly the answer is a resounding No! I say, no even though I went through Vietnam relatively unscathed. Even though I had an over 750 blood sugar count; that went into remission after injections of insulin. I don't feel unjustifiably lucky even though, as a side effect of a medication I was on, it cleared my vision for a good three years; even though I've worn glasses for forty-five years.

Sometimes I ask myself if I feel like a lucky punk knowing the answer is a resounding No! Why?

I'm glad you asked. I'll tell you why. I had a very serious drinking problem. I ate the grass in Vietnam. Ate it, and sucked it like farmers in the good old U.S. of A. Before I knew the meaning of the word: "D-e-f-o-l-i-e-n-t. Am I angry? No. Do I care? No. I ate a root in Vietnam. Sassafras. Imagine that. Most of my teeth are gone but I don't care. I'm unscathed. Tell that to some kid or mama San' in some "Ville" in "Country."

ONE TWO THREE

Some of us hardier souls are out here in mid-March. Oh we don't play like our bank rolls are on the line. We come out and play for myriad reasons. Exercise. Get out of the house. Earn respect. Get a good average. Maybe. I'm talking about why maybe up to twenty guys will brave still cold wind, hard ground, small crowds, to play baseball.

Why do we play baseball instead of going bowling? Instead of going somewhere and shooting pool? Working out in a gym?

Guess what sports fans? We play football, baseball, lacrosse. We work hard. Play hard. Live hard.

Local car races? Fishing tournaments? Skiing tryouts? We do it. Men and women. Girls and boys. We like competition. It's a vicarious thrill. Challenge.

And as with all things, there are changes. Sports announcers on TV. are speaking about baseball, now saying "It's a one, two, three, out inning..." If no one reaches base or scores. Well there's a little problem with that if you don't go back to saying; "One, two, three strikes, you're out!"

The problem is in the forgetting. Forgetting to announce these various plays could lead to trouble because if in a generation (twenty years), or two decades, (twenty years), someone pretends to have just thought to announce these "moves" or "plays" mayhem would reign.

"HUMM DINGER"

Hum dinger, Hum dinger, Hum dinger! It has been a long winter and we all had spring fever. Baseball. Fishing. Girls. Baseball. The guy on first base was taunting the pitcher.

I was on first base. Bill M. an average guy. I was trying to unnerve Joe R. the pitcher for the Greys. Maybe he'd offer up a home run or walk for my teammate Joe W. of the Hawks. A wild pitch would do too. I could run to second with my eyes closed against the catcher for the Greys, John S.

I was going to invoke "Tai-Chi."

"Center," I yelled. "Focus."

I was yelling to Joe W. the batter. I wanted Joe to drill one O.O.T.P. Oh. Oh. Tee. Pee. Out of the park. A slow curveball was coming up out of Joe R.'s right hand, a textbook perfect curveball for Joe W. He wasn't supposed to see it arcing down—maybe thinking the curveball was going to fall short or be "off the plate." Instead, he swung. He belted that ball for Chicago. It sailed out over the backfield fence and after nine innings, the Hawks won, 2-0. My and Joe W.'s runs.

2065

All I knew that summer was the healthy were healthy; the sick were damned. Pain was seen in the eyes of those in pain. There was screaming. You could tell the sick by the voices. Surly grunts. Growls. Nothing could be done. Nothing could control the spread of an infected area of skin to a normal area.

Phase 1. Immune

Suppress

Contain

Phase 2. Inoculate

Alleviate

Control

Phase 3. Deaden

Surround

Euthanize

And I still ask myself; "Could I really kill someone who

was begging to die?" I asked then, and ask now, before the first 100, 1,000, and after the first 100, 1,000 during the shrieking, howling, screaming? Are you aware what it is to deaden flesh so another part might survive? Alleviate or control pain with antibiotics and painkillers growing less and less available? Yes, 2065, as that particular disease was known, was a real killer.